THE TERRALIGHT

COLLECTION

PAMELA JEFFS

For the Battleaxe Inklings,
on Earth and in Valhalla.
Skol.

CONTENTS

SIX-GUN RECKONING

My true identity died long ago. I buried it with the husband-turned-vampire I was forced to slay and our daughter, whom he murdered. But the loss doesn't matter. A mother without her child is dead anyhow. And what better way to hide from grief than behind a new face and another name?

Doctor Abraham Van Helsing.

None need know the truth that their great defender is a woman beneath the men's clothes she wears.

I remove the envelope from my vest pocket. Much wrinkled, it rasps against my palm. I ease free the letter that found me in London not one month ago. The paper, a thick yellow sheet, is of fine quality.

Such richness is at odds with the rugged landscape I now travel. This wild, American West.

The mayor of Esperance has a neat cursive hand with letters heavy on the upstrokes. It reveals his character as one who is careful with decisions. I run through his words again. A mystery plagues his town. The circumstances, the mayor suggests, are supernatural. I press my lips together. I am not wholly convinced. But the victims are children, and so I shall investigate.

I rub a hand across my eyes. The trip has been long and I am weary. I press the letter and envelope back into my pocket and turn my attention outside the stagecoach. The incessant dust billows up in choking clouds as the steel-rimmed wheels bite into the uneven road. And the sunlight. In this country, it has an unfamiliar blue-white quality that causes the far distance to blur, losing itself to nothingness. I indulge a smile. Surely no vampire could survive out here.

But something does.

The letter in my pocket proves that no place is free of monsters.

The carriage driver yells, his voice roughened by dust. I lean out the window as we ease to a stop. I push the door open and step onto the gritty road, cursing as my boots, used to more civilised streets and pavements, gather dust on their gleaming tops.

The stage driver is not at his place on the box. But the guard man stands tall, shrewd eyes pinned on the plains and his shoulders tense. A rifle rests in the crook of his elbow. I ease around the side of the coach. The twin pairs of black horses stamp uneasily in their traces. I find the driver kneeling in the middle of the road.

'What is it? Why have we stopped?' I keep my hands close to the pistols concealed beneath my jacket. Highwaymen are a real threat.

The driver turns, face hidden in the shadow of his Stetson hat. His dusty, red bandana conceals the bottom half of his face, but his dark eyes catch mine.

'It's a young fella,' he says. 'A messenger, mebbe. Looks like 'e was thrown from his horse.' He flicks an uneasy glance up the track, but there is no sign of a lost beast.

The stricken figure lies face down in the middle of the road. I press a finger to his throat. A pulse flutters gently.

'Roll him over,' I direct.

The coachman obliges and the boy's face is revealed. Fair skin and slim features mark him as Caucasian—Irish maybe—if the red tint to his sandy blond hair is anything to go by. A forehead wound, edges ragged, crosses his right eyebrow. Clotted blood tracks down his cheek.

The driver flicks away a fly. He unclips a flask from his belt and dribbles a line of water across the boy's parched lips. They move slightly in response. His eyes open, bright blue.

I lean in. 'What is your name, boy?'

'Billy.' The words grate like sand over rock. His eyes close again.

The driver squints back up at me. 'He's just a kid. We ain't far from town and there's a doc set up there. Rear boot's clear. I'll strap 'im in.'

'Nonsense,' I say, straightening. 'Place him in the coach with me.'

'He's dirty and bloody, sir.'

'I insist.'

***

Esperance is a town built of bulldust, tumbleweeds and weathered lumber. It hunkers down, in a natural depression of the land, scowling like a grizzly bear. The stagecoach rumbles into the main street, scattering mangy dogs and young boys holding sticks like pistols. A blonde-haired woman in a blue dress watches us from the porch of a small house. She's young, but deep lines run from the sides of her nose to her mouth—the kind of lines that only true loss etches into someone's face. I recognise them from my own. I tip my finger to my hat, a small salute to her. The woman looks away.

From the seat opposite me, the young boy groans. His broad, shovel-like hands tenderly touch his forehead.

'Goddammit,' he mutters. 'Feels like I bin run over by a train.'

'At the very least,' I say, 'you fell off your horse.'

He rolls and sits himself up on his seat. I hand him a water flask. He takes a long draught and hands it back.

''T'weren't no horse.' He grins in a way that strikes me as a little forced. 'Just a lass's father who thought I was too handsy with 'is daughter.'

'I see.'

The boy grimaces. 'He gave me a good hidin' is all, and dumped me out there.'

'You're lucky he didn't kill you.'

Billy shrugs. Suddenly, he clutches at his empty gun holster and curses. 'Dammit. The old coot took my Colt.' His shoulders slump. 'I'm gonna have to steal me a new one now.'

'As I understand it, stealing can get you shot.'

'They gotta catch ya first.'

I chuckle. 'Indeed. So, you said your name is Billy?'

'Yep. Billy the Kid.'

'Sounds like an outlaw's name.'

'It sounds tough. Took me ages to pick it. So who are you, old man?'

I've spent many years pretending to be a man, so I am pleased. But old? I guess I would seem so to him. 'Abraham Van Helsing,' I say.

A spark of recognition usually presents when people hear my name but not this time.

'That ain't no name from 'round here. And your voice is different soundin' too. What's ya business here, Van Helsing?'

I smile. 'Would you believe me if I told you I was here to hunt monsters?'

Billy crosses his arms. 'What kinda monsters?'

'Ones that hurt good people.'

'So you're a bounty hunter, then?'

'Of a sort,' I reply, 'but not the kind you think. I don't hunt humans. I'm after real monsters. The kind that hide in the night.'

The young man settles back in his seat. 'In this country, that don't mean you're not hunting men.'

'Would you be interested in helping me, Billy?'

'What you got in mind?'

I press a finger to my lips and feign thinking. 'Let's say I buy you a gun and you work for me while I'm here.'

Billy leans forward and spits in his palm.

He holds it out. 'A new gun and I'm yours.'

***

The doctor is in the saloon, a drunken man who tends to Billy with shaking hands. The cut on the boy's head, once cleaned, is not as bad as it looked. A bandage and shot of whiskey, as payment for services rendered, and the boy is ready for work.

He stands next to me, leaning against the bar, all swagger and confidence. I signal the saloonkeeper, a green-eyed woman with rich, red hair. More Irish blood in this backwater place.

'Two shots of whiskey, please,' I say.

She nods and places the glasses on the countertop. As she reaches for the bottle, her sleeves fall back to reveal forearms terribly scarred. She catches me looking.

'The marks of bad men,' she says, in a broad Irish drawl. 'Those who like to cut women.' Her nostrils widen for second as if she's scenting the air. She places the bottle back down. 'But you ain't a *man* like that, are you?'

The hair rises on my neck. For an instant I wonder if she suspects the truth about me. I swallow the shot, relishing the scorch of fiery liquid in my throat. My glass returns to the scarred bar with a *clink.* 'Of course not, good lady. Women should, in my experience, be respected.'

'You show me a respectful man and I'll show you the second coming of the good lord Jesus Christ.'

The saloonkeeper extends her hand. The callused skin of her palm catches against my fingers as I grasp it.

'Name's Grace O'Conner,' she says. 'Welcome to Esperance.'

'Thank you, Ms. O'Conner.'

I place a coin on the bar and she snatches it up. Next to me, Billy downs his shot.

'I am looking for the mayor,' I say.

Grace's countenance darkens. 'So he's the one that brought you here?'

'Yes, good lady.'

She sniffs. 'Over next to the marshal's office.'

***

The half-doors creak as I push them open. The smell of hot earth and dried grass fills the air. It's a relief to be free of the stifling heat of the saloon proper. Billy sticks to my heels, busy inspecting the second-hand six-gun I bought for him off a cowboy inside.

'Hey, Boss,' says Billy, looking up. He touches his bloodstained collar. 'Mind if I head home for a bit? Wanna change and let my ma know I'm okay. She'll be worried about me.'

'Of course,' I say. 'I'll meet you outside the mayor's when I'm done.'

The boy scampers off, whippet fast, and disappears down the main street. He's small, but wiry and quick. Thoughts of apprenticing him take seed. He would make an excellent vampire hunter.

The marshal's office is across the way and several doors down. Two deputies occupy the veranda, leaning against the doorposts with hands loose and eyes sharp. Next to the rugged building is a more decorative place. Fine curtains show behind the glazed windows, and a red painted sign over the porch declares *Office of Mayor Tommin.*

I step out into the dusty street, again lamenting the abuse to my boots. I really should have worn something more serviceable. I pause as a tumbleweed sails by, skipping over a pile of horse dung as it goes. Twenty more steps and I reach the mayor's office.

I knock and Tommin answers: a haggard man upon whom the mantle of office weighs heavy. Or is it some other weight? He grasps my hand in both of his as he welcomes me.

'Doctor Van Helsing? Thank you. Thank you for coming.'

'Of course. My pleasure.'

He directs me to his desk where two plush chairs wait, their fine detailing at odds with the rough-hewn plank walls. On his desk sits a pile of the same yellow paper as the letter that brought me here. I take a seat.

The mayor sits opposite. Silent, he seems to gather his thoughts. I wait as a fly buzzes in the front window and a clock ticks, monotone, over the door. The room smells slightly of fine tobacco and whiskey. Tommin then rubs a hand through his grease-black hair. His grey eyes flick up, clouded with unease.

He pushes a newspaper across his desk towards me.

'The latest death, Doctor.'

I glance down. The front page glares at me, or more so, the illustration on the front. It's the face of a child, a boy of around thirteen years.

The mayor shakes his head. 'Joseph McCarty was his name. You may have seen his mother, Catherine, on your way in. The lady in the blue dress. She's not accepted he's gone and has spent the last week on her porch waiting for him to return.'

He presses his fingers to the bridge of his nose and takes a deep breath. 'It's a terrible business, burying children,' he says, 'and we have had our fill. Six dead in the last month. We can't catch the culprit.'

I look away from the newspaper. 'The children. Only boys, or girls also?'

'Five boys, one girl.'

'And the deaths?' I ask. 'The manner of and details are the same for all?'

'Yes.' The mayor shudders. 'And those details are what have set our town doctor to drinking.' He blinks. 'The kids when we find them are all sucked dry. Bloodless.'

My mind races. An American vampire? My thoughts run from Native American skinwalkers to the *Tah-tah-kle'-ah* Owl Witches. But no, something tells me this is more personal—a white man's monster.

I push the paper back along the table.

'I think I can help,' I say. 'Tonight, I'll begin the hunt.'

***

All but one of the bodies were found in a gully just beyond the outskirts of town. When I arrive, just on the edge of dusk when the light is gold and the sky a bruised purple, I find Catherine McCarty there. Still in her blue dress, she is a light-grey shadow against the sunset. Her eyes are trained on the far horizon.

Distant.

Longing.

I place my weapons satchel on the ground and approach her.

'I know my Joseph is gone,' she says, her voice a whisper, 'and that they all say I'm crazy. Truth is, I'm waiting for the creature to return. I want retribution.'

My long-scarred, female heart breaks for this woman. The desire for revenge resonates. Even after these long years, I would kill and kill again the vampire that infected my husband and stole my family from me. I swallow back the old grief—swallow and push it back down to the dark place just below my heart.

'Go home, my dear,' I say through gritted teeth. 'I'll avenge your son and pray it gives you some solace.'

The woman laughs. A dry, brittle sound.

She turns, her gaze bitter. 'Yes. Send the little woman home. You men are all the same. You will never understand what it means for a woman to lose her child.'

There is no way to console her without revealing myself, so I withhold further words. Her face twists and she gathers her skirts. As she sweeps by me, I forgive her anger.

This, too, is something I understand.

With her exit, so falls away the sunlight. The moon rises, peeking over the horizon with her yellow-cheese face, sombre. Billy arrives from town and drops a bundle of wood, the sticks clacking together like bones. He kneels to arrange them.

'No need, my boy,' I say. 'We'll not require a fire tonight. It's the dark and shadows for us.'

Billy frowns. 'You ain't serious. It's damnable cold out here at night. Wind off the plains cuts right through ya.'

'I understand, but it is necessary. Blood-drinkers usually fear the light. If this creature is anything like the others I hunt abroad, then we must give it the cover of night.'

'Well, I guess it's plain bread for supper, then.'

'And no hot tea either, unfortunately.'

Billy grins and pulls a flask out of his vest pocket. 'Nuthin' to fear. I got something stronger to keep us company.'

I roll my eyes and open my bag. Within it, the tools of my trade are carefully stowed. My crossbow and stakes soaked in garlic oil. Ampoules of holy water and rows of gleaming bullets. I unholster the twin pistols from my belt. Their black iron barrels gleam darker than the night. Blessed by priests of ten different religions, they are the most versatile of my weapons.

'They're fine guns,' says Billy, sitting gnawing on a chunk of bread. 'You any good at shootin' 'em?'

'Not too bad,' I say with a shrug.

The night eases on, and with it comes the chill wind that Billy promised. We sit in the dark, our backs against a boulder.

'Tell me, Van Helsing,' says Billy. 'How does one come into your line of work?'

'Necessity.'

'So there's a fair amount of monsters in your country?'

'You could say that.'

'And you like protecting people?'

The faces of my husband and daughter, the first of those I cared about lost to monsters, float before me.

'Someone must do it.'

His questions are probing too close to old wounds, so I ask one of my own.

'What work do you do?'

He shrugs. 'A bit o' this and that. Not much in the protecting people kinda business.'

He sounds regretful for some reason. Maybe the boy has secrets to hide too.

'Is your work of the legal kind?' I ask.

'Sometimes.' He rolls the cylinder of his revolver, the noise spinning off into the night.

I look away. 'Well, all I know is that whatever you do, it should always be to try and better the lives of others.'

The clicking sound of Billy's gun dies away.

A sharp cry from out across the plain replaces it.

Then a laugh, high and thin.

'What the holy hell was that?' says Billy.

'Our quarry, I'd wager.'

I get to my feet, pulling Billy up with me. The moon hangs high above us, her full face lighting the prairie. In the near distance, a flash of white catches my attention.

Another cry.

A child.

And a creature rides his tail.

She floats above the ground, a dress of black silk billowing out behind her. Her teeth, long and pointed, gleam against the porcelain of her skin. Hair, red as fire, writhes like vipers around her face. And her eyes, poison green and glowing, are a predator's in the moonlight.

It's the saloonkeeper.

Grace O'Conner.

So not an American vampire at all.

An Irish one.

One who specifically hunts males.

One who doesn't fear the sun.

She is the dreaded *Dearg-Due*.

The boy she hunts runs panicked before her. I recognise him as one playing in the street earlier today. I grab my crossbow and throw one of my pistols to Billy.

'Use mine. The bullets in it are blessed. Wait until she's close. Aim for her heart,' I say.

But the young man stands pinned to the spot, gaze fixed upon the creature.

'Billy. The gun!' I bark.

He blinks and nods. His hand snaps up, pistol aimed.

The hunted child makes the mistake of glancing over his shoulder. A bush, unseen, rises before him and he tumbles face down into the dirt. Grace pounces, but before she bites, I release a bolt. My aim is off and it slams into her shoulder.

'Damn,' I hiss.

The vampiress scowls and claws the bolt free. The boy at her feet scuttles away. He heads for town—for safety.

Her attention is not on him anymore.

She glides forward. A vision painted in tones of red, ivory and ebony.

The rent in the fabric at her shoulder shows a hole in her pale skin, but no blood.

'Van Helsing,' she says, her voice poisoned honey. 'Why would you stop me?'

I cock the crossbow again. 'It is my job.'

She smiles and the tips of her teeth press against her blood-red lips. 'But these boys. They grow into men.' She holds out her scarred arms, the raised ridges glistening in the moonlight. 'And see the ruin such men wreak on women.'

'I cannot deny it,' I say, 'but revenge taken upon the young will change nothing.'

'I need only stop one, Van Helsing, to make a difference. It took only one man to break my spirit as a girl. One to slice these cuts into my arms just to see me bleed, and only one for me to choose to slit my wrists and be reborn, monstrous.'

I imagine her fresh corpse clawing its way clear of her grave and shudder. The story she tells holds true with the mythology I know of her creation. The men of her time did not treat her kindly.

Grace's eye roves to Billy. 'Just like your companion. Such a bonny Irish boy. He looks so innocent, does he not, standing there with his pistol trained upon me?'

'He's here to protect children.'

The vampiress throws her head back and laughs—a chiming of musical notes, sharp edges like shattered glass. 'Yon Billy the Kid, a good man? Have you asked yourself why you found him as you did? Why he was in the middle of the road?'

I glance at Billy. His focus is trained on the woman.

'Could you imagine perhaps that he hurt a poor girl?' she continues. 'A poor Irish girl?'

Billy's hands start trembling.

'Did he tell you that he robbed a train and kidnapped her for a ransom? And when her dear pappy couldn't pay, Billy left her tied up, cut and bleeding, to draw in the coyotes.' Grace lifts her chin. 'Her blood drew me to her. I put her out of her misery. She died, begging me to hunt him down. Your outlaw friend there is what young boys grow into!'

Her voice rings with conviction.

'Is it true, Billy?' I ask.

'She's lying!' he snarls.

But the pitch of his voice betrays him.

I lower the cross bolt. 'Ah, Billy.'

I turn to the vampiress. 'Why didn't you kill him on the road?'

'The sun rose before I finished. With it my human form and conscience are returned to me. Only in the dark do I have the strength to kill.'

'You know I must stop you, Grace.'

'Give me your murderous offsider and I'll move on from this town.'

'No.' I shake my head. 'You will not be the one to judge nor punish this boy for his crimes.'

'Then we are done speaking!'

Grace launches for Billy. The boy panics. His first shot flies wide, his second catches Grace's cheek, the blessed steel splitting the skin into a black line.

She screeches and catches his neck in a two-handed grip. Her black gown flares wide, encasing them both in a dark cocoon. Billy falls. His gun skitters away across the ground.

Grace strikes.

Billy screams.

I kick at the woman, my boot connecting with flesh as hard as iron.

She lifts her head, chin dripping scarlet with Billy's blood. 'He tastes sweet!'

Billy moans.

My first crossbow bolt hits her between the eyes. She rears back, breast exposed. A practiced motion and another bolt is cocked and fired.

It shears straight through her heart.

She slumps over Billy, long red tresses splayed out across his chest. She coughs. Her luminous gaze, now dimmed, finds mine. 'You of all people…' Another cough. 'As a woman, you should have understood…'

Her form fractures into dust and crumbles away in the evening breeze. I drop the bow and run to Billy's side. His breath shudders.

'She was right. I've done bad things,' he whispers. 'I've hurt all kinds of folk.'

'I'm sorry you did that.'

'Me too.'

I place a hand on the boy's forehead. The mother in me can't help but wish to ease his pain.

'I'm sorry, Billy, but she's bitten you.'

His hand reaches for his throat. 'Yeah. Hurts like hell.'

'It's her venom burning through you. Soon, you will turn and become a vampire like she was.'

'Can ya stop it?'

'Not without ending your life.'

Billy looks past me, gaze trained towards the stars. 'I deserve it, I reckon. Do what ya gotta do.'

He grasps my hand. 'Make it quick?'

'I will.'

I lift the last of my cross bolts and hold it over his heart. He nods and grimaces. His teeth have already lengthened. I ready myself. Killing this young boy makes me no better than the *Dearg-Due*. I'm no less a monster. A tear crawls from the corner of my eye.

But it must be done.

A sharp crack reverberates down the gully and pain blossoms in the centre of my back.

I tumble sideways to the ground, stunned.

A shadow approaches. A woman in a blue dress. Catherine McCarty. The gun Billy dropped—my gun—is still smoking in her hand.

'I've already lost one son,' she snarls. 'You'll not take my last.'

'Ma, NO!' cries Billy.

But Catherine aims.

The barrel is set between my eyes.

And the crack of the shot, before darkness falls,
roars thunderous.

MIRRORVERSE

I can hear the engines through the mirror, their rattle and their hum. But for the first time since I left Earth, I detect something different in the sound. The rhythm of their song has changed—and change is a problem when it comes to the engines.

I take one last look at the mirrorverse I'm visiting, the rust-coloured sunset settling over a restless Pacific Ocean. Everything looks and sounds sharp edged, as if cast from crystal: the waves crashing on the shore and brittle chime of sand shifting. But the foam and salt tingling against my toes feels real. This is my favourite Earth memory, and I enter the mirror at precisely 17:00 hours every day to visit it.

It helps with the loneliness, with the homesickness.

But the engines are still calling.

I turn away from the scene and face the mirror at my back. The silvered glass is the portal back to the real world. From this side, I can see my reality—see into my ship, see the outline of the gantry—but the edges are blurred. Whenever looking back into the real world, it always seems flat and manufactured to me.

But that's the trick of the mirror, the lure to try to make you stay.

I twist the dial on my wrist-portal. The semi-transparent surface of the mirror shivers before turning fluid. I step through, feeling the separated molecules clutch at my sleeves as I pass.

Momentarily disorientated, I close my eyes and count a full twenty seconds before my head stops reeling. I push aside my unease. Has it always taken that long for me to recover, or does it seem to get longer the more times I visit each mirrorverse?

Reality beckons. The room sharpens into focus. It looks the same as I left it, the flat metal sheets fronted by hanging racks from which a thousand mirrors hang. Memory Mirrors. Created with experimental, offshoot string theory technology, manufactured by Australian scientists to be the repository of humanity's collective memory.

America sent me—Commander Jane Everton—the last astronaut alive, on the last shuttle ever built, into space to save them.

And saved they were. I just couldn't get to the survivor station built to receive them on Mars. I escaped the planet's atmosphere only to have the guidance systems fail. So I orbited and from my vantage point, I saw everything. I saw the beginning of the nuclear war, watched as the lights of Earth flickered out not long after that.

And now I travel the universe. Aimless. Alone.

Hoping for a miracle.

My boots clang against the mesh floor as I head for the far end of the gallery. The ship's electric lights blaze overhead, powered by the external solar array. I pass by a mirror that reveals a blurred school of Koi fish swimming in a pond, and then another one with an aviary filled with watercolour-painted parrots. The exit is just beyond.

The door slides open silently on my approach. I step into the ship's main corridor. Any serenity gained from my evening visit to the ocean is lost in an instant.

Breach alarms are blaring, red lights cycling overhead. The monotone computer voice is droning over the speakers.

'*Hull breach, Sector Twelve airlock. Engine speed reduced. Prepare for sector shutdown and purge.*'

Sector Twelve. That's the Mirror Gallery.

Purge?

Shit!

I spin on my heel and race back through the door. The engines whine in protest as the computer drops off more speed. At least there is nothing wrong with the engines.

But the purge is a problem.

When the doors open, the mirrors will be sent into space.

I skid to a stop at a control console by the Koi Pond Mirror. The screen reveals that the doors to all other sectors have been sealed. I am trapped here.

Frantically I tap in a sequence of commands. My fingernails click against the yellow illuminated buttons. But I am too late. I can't stop the computer's auto-commands. The vents at the far end of the gallery open. A hiss of atmospheric pressure releases into the airlock. The outer airlock's doors begin the sequence to unlock, confirmed by the sound of grating gears in the outer hull wall.

'*Artificial gravity terminated for purge…*' drones the computer.

'Dammit!' My feet leave the gantry. I grab for the Koi Pond Mirror, but my fingers slip on the slick frame. I float backwards and then stop, spinning in a slow circle a metre above the floor, unable to reach a mirror. The grind of the airlock doors intensifies, and so does my pulse. I'm almost out of time.

I think of my mother.

I think of my father.

If there's an afterlife, it will be good to see them again.

But my circling motion is elliptical. Another revolution and a mirror swings into view, almost within reach. Its surface ripples with the blurred outlines of a yellow and blue landscape. The Savannah Mirror. I reach out, fingers spread-eagled and desperate to reach the frame.

Almost.

I circle again.

This time I catch it.

The airlock doors start beeping.

'Purge imminent. Countdown commenced. Three...two...one...'

With a desperate sob, I twist my wrist-portal. The mirror shivers, and I am sucked through.

***

All the noise of the alarms, the grinding and the hissing, has gone. There is only the sound of the breeze, a breeze that smells of dry grass and wild, sun-drenched places. I turn to look back at the mirror.

The surface is a shifting plane of silver and black. The blurred view in it swings, showing a cloud of glittering mirrors hanging in the darkness of space: the collected history of humanity, adrift. The surfaces of each mirror flash as they slowly twist, catching briefly the light of the ancient stars that they float amongst. The picture of a retreating ship swings into view and then passes again. My ship, my home—out of reach.

I fall to my knees, feeling the long, yellow crystalline grass shatter beneath them with the impact. Gone. The ship is gone…

I press my fists to my eyes. Heat stings the back of them but I refuse to let myself cry. A scream builds in my chest, but I refuse to let that out also. Instead I cling to anger. I let it manifest and fill the hole in my heart. I suck in a shuddering breath. I push myself up and brush my trembling hands down the front of my pants. Let's see what this mirrorverse has to offer. Let's see if there is any way for the living to survive here.

The grass brushes my thighs as I walk towards the only landmark on the empty plain: a tall baobab tree. Its stumpy, skeletal arms reach up to embrace the impossibly blue sky. Not a cloud mars the horizon, leaving the bright jewel-like sun to blaze down upon me. Its heat is real against the back of my neck. I instantly feel thirsty.

I reach back and unclip my water bottle from my standard-issue space station utility belt. But I have forgotten to fill it. Three drops of water trickle down my throat, barely chasing away the dryness.

There is a waterhole by the tree. The shallow dam, showing no evidence of animal life, curves past the stout trunk of the baobab. The silence of the place confirms the unnatural nature of the landscape. I look at the coffee-coloured water. I have never tried to eat or drink anything in the mirrorverses before. But I am so thirsty. I kneel down by the edge and dip my water bottle in.

The water moves differently than it does in reality. Instead of bubbling as it fills the bottle, it chimes in a series of increasing musical notes. *Ting, ting, ting... ting. A, B, C—G.*

The sound is lyrical. I pull the water bottle up and place the rim of it against my lips and swallow.

It's like drinking air. There is no substance to the water, no satisfaction in the consumption of it. Disappointed, I empty the remaining liquid out. It splashes into the dust, again with high-toned musical overtures.

A, B, C—G.

Another sound catches my attention: the cracking of brittle grass and the deep thud of a bass-line footstep. I turn and scan the shrubbery.

Nothing.

Then something.

A lioness.

So something does live here. I watch as the lean creature stalks out past the closest shrub. Her long black claws click against the sun-hardened ground, their lengths glistening, glass-like, in the bright sunlight. I remember seeing lions back on Earth. Here in the mirrorverse, the differences are striking. The savage beasts of reality—all smooth muscle, teeth, and fierce dispositions—are nothing in comparison to the memory the mirror holds of them.

This lioness is crystalline—all angles, sharp edged and razor-like. Her body is semi-transparent, the clear facets of it imbued with gold highlights.

Her eyes, two backlit emeralds, are fixed on me. She does not seem impressed with my intrusion in her territory. A low growl, threatening, rumbles in her throat—a sound like a glass chandelier chiming.

I glance around, looking for a weapon. Nearby, half-buried in the dust, is a fist-sized rock. I sidle over to it.

The lioness snarls, the black line of her lips peeling back to reveal her ivory teeth.

'You want a piece of me?' I snarl back.

I lunge for the rock and feel its bulk against my palm. Across from me the lioness leaps, her ears pressed flat to her head, her long claws extended.

I pull back my arm to aim. I throw.

She is mid-air when the rock connects.

There is the sound of glass cracking.

Where the rock strikes her chest, fractures appear, long white scars.

The lioness falls short, a deep, musical G-note sounding out as her feet hit the ground. She skids on her haunches, a high C-note of sound as her claws rake up dust. Then she slides to a stop. Her teeth are still bared, her claws still extended.

She's injured but has retained her weapons, and I unfortunately have nothing else to throw.

The animal rises to her feet. She growls again, that low rumble, and begins to walk towards me. She intends to keep fighting, but her smooth gait is marred. She is limping.

And there is something obscene about her ruined perfection. Suddenly I am ashamed. I have damaged her, broken her. And for what? To save my own life?

What life?

Without a ship and trapped here in the mirrorverse, there is not much chance left of living.

The anger that's been holding me upright suddenly fades. My shoulders slump and I bow my head. I wait for the inevitable strike, but it doesn't come.

I look up. The lioness has halted three paces away from me. Her teeth are hidden but there is tension in the lines of her stance. There is also something else. It's like she's waiting—waiting to see what my next move will be.

What to do?

Fight or run?

I am too weary to do either. I sit down on the ground and stare at her. She really is beautiful in a fierce, fragile kind of a way.

And she is alone, just like me.

The thought comes out of nowhere. I recall the lack of animal tracks near the water and the profound silence of this mirrorverse. She is alone here. In that second something shifts in me. A desire forms, immediate and sudden, to bond with the animal. I don't belong in this place, there is nothing here to help me survive—and if I am going to die, I don't want to do it alone.

If only I could befriend this lioness. Somehow tame her.

I look at the cracks in her chest. Brute force is not the way. So I swallow my fear and raise my arm hesitantly, palm open, fingers outstretched.

This heartfelt plea for compassion is now my weapon, instead of any defence offered by a rock.

The lioness follows the movement of my hand. Slowly, her ears rise from her scalp and press forward in curiosity.

She moves a step closer. I do not dare to break eye contact with her as she stretches her muzzle forward to test my scent.

Another step. She is only inches away. I swallow; the fear of losing my hand to her teeth overwhelms me. My fingers begin to tremble—

But the great lioness chooses otherwise. With gentle intent, she presses her nose into my palm.

I let out the breath I hadn't realised I was holding. Success.

But my moment of relief dissolves as a sharp, sudden pain tears at my stomach. I gasp, doubling over. The lioness moves away—only a few paces, though. She sits as if to wait, her manner calm.

***

My blood is on fire. I am blind and all I can hear are my own screams. The ground is at my back and I have a dim awareness of the lioness sitting at my side. I am thankful for her presence, thankful for her quiet strength in these last moments.

***

Hours have passed and I am still not dead. My vision is starting to clear; the pain is beginning to subside. But I am still weak. I will lie here just a little longer. I feel so thirsty.

***

I suspect it is the water that did it. The mirrorverse water I drank earlier. How long ago was that? I am not sure. Time moves differently, if at all, in this place.

I lift my hands. They are sharp edged now and semi-transparent. They have a certain beauty to them when they catch the sunlight and gleam a fresh pink colour, a similar shade to what my skin used to be.

My lioness is by my side. Her fractured chest has healed and now she is as tame as a kitten. Her head is pressed into my newly made, crystalline palm. She has come with me to farewell my past—to welcome me to my new future in the mirrorverse with her.

We stand together before the mirror. As I look out onto the dark universe beyond its surface, I find it to be a cold contrast to the savannah I now reside in.

I look down at the rock in my hand. It feels heavy. It will do the job nicely.

'Time to end it,' I whisper, the words sliding off my lips in a falling scale of musical B notes. The lioness yawns in response.

Yes. It's time. I pull my arm back and aim. A chorus of discordant musical notes erupts as the rock hits its mark. The mirror-doorway to my old reality shatters, sending a thousand shards falling into the yellow grass.

I can't help but feel a certain satisfaction in seeing the end of my past. I place my hand on the lioness's head.

'Let's head back,' I say. 'I'm feeling thirsty again.'

In Opposition to the Foe

The rainforest whispers in a language all its own. Its voice is the drip-drop patter of water to the leaf-littered earth and the cackle of bright-breasted parrots in the canopy. But danger covets the cloak of the forest's dense skirts. It lurks hidden, concealing the wicked teeth and misshapen bodies of those human mutations created in the buru labs but deemed not worthy. The aliens sent their abominations into the wilderness to die. But humans are strong. Even corrupted, they proved stronger than their creators gave them credit for.

Now, they roam.

They hunt.

And they should be feared, but I'll brave them today. For word runs hot over the buru comms channels. The aliens are planning a search. Unguarded tech rests out here somewhere.

Whispers of a wreck.

A ship I can, maybe, use against the invaders.

I push open the access hatch leading out from the ancient WW2 bunker. The wild ginger clump concealing the entrance parts as the door swings on well-oiled hinges. I step clear. The light is filtered green and the air smells clean outside. Not like the damp, musty corridors below; corridors filled with everything I own—supplies and munitions. I glance back. It's not much, but it keeps me safe and it's a place to call home.

Home.

More like just walls and a roof built from the ruins of our invaded civilisation. But it's all I have left.

No, not quite all.

I glance up. Soleil is where she always is, sleeping in the branches of the tallest tree. As much as I've tried, she refuses to join me below ground. Her eagle head is tucked tight beneath her shining wing and her lion body disappears into the shadows of dense leaves behind. She looks every part a griffin from legend. My heart clenches. As always, I can't help but remember all she was, and that which she no longer is.

If only I had been braver. If only I'd left my hiding place when she screamed for me.

Her true voice still rings in my mind—

Aster! Help me!

What I wouldn't give to change the past. But I can only influence the future. Only protect her as best I can.

I whistle low. Soleil responds, head emerging and bright eagle eyes blinking. She tips off her branch and glides to the ground. I rest a hand on her beak. She keens quietly in greeting.

'Ready to hunt?' I ask, knowing she understands me but cannot answer.

She tilts her head and her golden eye swivels to mine—an eye weighted with the wisdom only a human soul can own; a human soul tied to a mutated form. I sense her eagerness.

I holster my pump-action shotgun across my back and check my ammo belt. On one hip hangs my grandfather's xiphos. The old man gifted the ancient Greek blade to me when we brought Soleil home. Both were my responsibility now.

'Let's go then.'

***

The forest never welcomes. It despises our presence here, holding its secrets close. I press forward into the sombre wall of green and black. The vegetation parts reluctantly around me. Spikes pluck at my shirt and the rotting stench of carrion flowers fills my nostrils. I flick away an offending fly and shoulder my way past a dense curtain of broad-leafed vines. Soleil follows, her cat-like reflexes gifting her silence as she moves through the undergrowth.

A branch creaks.

No sounds are accidental in this place. I ease my loaded shotgun free from the gun slip. The xiphos remains in its scabbard. That's for close fighting and I'm hoping it won't come to that.

Another creak.

My gaze snaps up.

The forest canopy falls silent.

I stretch an arm wide across Soleil's chest. Her wings flare as she shoves her feathered breast against me. Then she stops also, her neck arched back.

We both sense it.

Something approaches.

I lick my lips. A beat of sweat slides down my neck and a mosquito whines by my ear. I glance at Soleil. Her gaze is fixed on the trees.

Snap.

Crack.

The forest erupts.

I squeeze the trigger and the shotgun roars, recoiling through my shoulder. The stench of gunfire chokes the air. The shot hits its mark. A peacock-scaled, half-serpent, half-human female falls from a tree, screaming. Her sibilant cry, slithering from a fanged mouth, burbles away, drowned in the blood-soaked ruin of her lungs. She lands with a muted *thump*, curled auburn hair a shock of colour splayed like a carrion flower across the undergrowth. Her viper tail thrashes, scattering leaf litter and gore.

Two more creatures follow. First, a male with muscled forearms and the wicked glare of a deranged psychotic. He aims for Soleil. Her battle cry cuts the air in a shriek that speaks of high places and quick kills. She launches, wings raised and talons extended.

The last creature is mine. I fire. And again. The trigger clicks. *Damn.* Gun's jammed. But my attacker's been hit—left arm bleeding. He snarls, venom on his lips. He isn't ready to end this fight yet. I toss the firearm aside. I'll get it back later. The xiphos rings clear of its scabbard—

But the mutant has already crossed the distance. No room for me to swing. He lunges and the flat of my double-edged blade slaps against his chest. He drives me down, coiling his sleek tail to pin my legs. This close, his hot breath smells of rot and sulphurous venom. Clawed fingers find my throat and squeeze. A grip like iron. My gritted teeth slip and cut my tongue and I taste blood. My lungs burn. I buck and push harder on the blade, trying to twist it—trying to cut the scaled chest pressing down on me. The viper-man's mouth widens, fangs just a handspan from my shoulder.

This is a stupid way to die.

A stupid place to die.

The soundtrack of Soleil's battle plays somewhere behind me. Hisses versus eagle cry.

'Hih! Hih!'

A stranger's voice.

The pressure on my neck eases. A trickle of air rakes its way into my lungs. I cough. The mutant looks up and away. His features change—a predator suddenly made prey.

He slithers off me. With a flick of his tail he retreats, scaling the nearest tree and disappearing into the canopy. Nearby, the rustle of leaves betrays the departure of Soleil's opponent. I lie on the rich-smelling ground, exhausted. Soleil, breathing heavily, moves to stand over me, her stance tense. She cries out a challenge.

I sit up. Everything hurts.

And I see him.

In the clearing with a worn blaster held in one hand and my shotgun in the other.

A buru.

Shit.

***

The buru points both weapons down and away. A sign of peace? Impossible. His kind doesn't collaborate. They care only for the conquering of planets and the mutation of any native species. Universal domination is their aim.

I keep my blade raised.

The alien moves forward with languid grace—long-limbed and lithe with blue dreadlocks coiling past his gold-skinned cheeks and over his shoulders. His eyes are the cruel doorways to his soul, solid orbs of scarlet red.

He points to Soleil. 'How did you tame that griffinous?'

I've never heard a buru speak before. Heavily accented, he sounds something almost between a Greek and French person trying to speak English.

'She's got a name. Soleil.'

His chin tilts. 'Soleil. How is it she is so quiet?'

I can't tell him even if I wanted to. She has always been that way around me, like I tether her to reality or the past, somehow. 'She's special.'

He moves closer still, a cautious step—the type you take when approaching a wild animal. His black metal armour seems to soak up the light.

'Were either of you bitten?' he asks. 'I can help you, if you will let me.'

My hand tightens around the hilt of my blade. 'You help us, Buru?'

The alien's thin lips quirk up. 'I have a name, also. Dinuth.'

'I don't care.'

'Perhaps you should. Some say I am special too.'

I get to my knees. 'I don't believe you.'

But before Dinuth answers, Soleil stumbles. Her legs crumble and her head collides with the ground.

'NO!' I cry, scrabbling to her. Froth bubbles from her beak and her gaze roams wildly, following shadows that don't exist. The buru appears by her head. He runs a long fingered hand over her beak and down her neck. His blood-coloured eyes flick to mine.

'She's been bitten. Viperion venom will kill her within the hour unless you let me help her.'

Viperions. So that's what his kind calls those human-snake hybrids.

'You bastards made those things.'

'Yes. But I can save her from them, too.'

I glare at him then look back at Soleil.

I can't help her.

But maybe he can.

'She dies and I'll kill you. You hand us over to other buru to experiment on and I kill you.'

Dinuth moves to my side and hands my shotgun over. 'We are without issue then, for I have no desire to depart this life, I assure you.'

***

Dinuth leads me deeper than I have ever gone into the forest. At over seven feet tall, he is plenty strong enough to carry Soleil. Still unconscious, she hangs draped over his shoulder, her avian head bumping gently against his back. I'm reminded of a chicken I saw as a child—a bird with a broken neck strung up on a line and swaying in the wind.

The forest floor gives way to bog, and the trees here show signs of dying—withered leaves on finger-like twigs and bark peeling away to reveal silvered heartwood. The stink of decaying vegetation rises around me, a miasma that clings like a damp, mouldy shirt. My boots mire in black mud, but it doesn't seem to slow Dinuth. Head down, he's on a mission and it's my problem to keep up. My bruised throat aches as I suck in urgent breaths.

The tree trunks grow blacker. The smell grows worse and then the forest parts.

The buru pauses at the edge of a dark lake. An errant breeze ruffles from across the water to kiss my brow, carrying with it the scent of stagnant salt. Dead trees circle the bank—white, skeletal limbs frozen in the rictus of death. But the black and white landscape pales in comparison to that which lies half-submerged in the lake.

A wreck, ten stories tall.

It's all that remains of a buru scientific cruiser.

I've seen what they do in those transports…and it's the same type of cruiser I saved Soleil from.

A chill crawls up my spine.

Nothing about this is good.

The visible portion of the ship's hull towers over water that reflects like a mirror. A rusted metal skin, pitted with corrosion, rolls over the ship's hollow bones. Ragged holes, bitter eyes of darkness, mar the structure just above the waterline.

'There is no way we are going in there.'

Dinuth turns. His brow furrows. 'My workshop is inside. What we need to save her is there.'

'This is a buru science facility.'

'Once perhaps. Not now.'

I rest a hand on the pommel of my xiphos. 'I'm not an idiot. Soleil and I go in there, we don't come out the same.'

The alien's gaze flicks to my hand then back. He shakes his head. 'This facility was destroyed by a storm many years ago. The other buru have since dismissed it. You are safe here.'

'No, we are not. I heard them on the comms. They're looking for this place.'

Again, Dinuth shakes his head. 'No. They seek a different fallen ship. One that malfunctioned two days ago and fell closer to the ocean.'

So, this isn't the wreck I was chasing.

'Please,' says Dinuth, voice anxious. 'This delay may cost your friend her life.'

I glare at him. 'She isn't my friend. She's my sister—or what your people left of her.'

The lines of Dinuth's face deepen. His eyes lower a moment, long black lashes brushing his cheek. He clears his throat.

'A sibling, you say? And one with close matching DNA, I'd hazard.'

'We are—were—twins,' I admit.

'Rare,' says Dinuth. 'An important discovery. Interesting, though, that you were kept human and they changed her.'

'They didn't do it on purpose. I was never captured. Soleil was.'

Dinuth frowns, eyes full of pity I don't need from the likes of him.

'I see,' he says. 'Still, fascinating that your familial connection was enough to keep her tame. Most others...' He glances at the forest. '...turn to madness. She is a perfect specimen.'

'Specimen?' I spit. 'She was a perfect human being!'

Dinuth's lips press thin. 'And perhaps she can be again. Come. Let me show you.'

I clench my teeth and consider pulling my blade as he presses two fingers to his lips. A long, low whistle echoes across the lake.

'Look,' he whispers, pointing to the wrecked ship.

A small, white face appears at the lower edge of the largest hole in the ship's hull. The child waves a hand and then disappears.

An undeniably human hand.

An unbound human on a buru ship?

My curiosity is piqued. Humans are never allowed to roam free around buru. I'd raided enough ships in my search to find Soleil to know. I've seen terrible things. Humans chained and experimented on; the savageness of the resulting abominations— creatures I have no names for.

'Will you trust me or let your sister die?' asks Dinuth.

Soleil stirs on his shoulder and falls limp again.

I have no choice. 'Trust? Never. But for my sister's sake, I'll come.'

'Good.'

Dinuth presses a button on the inside of his armoured wrist. The edge of the lake boils in response. Black, stinking sediment rises, coiling just beneath the surface of the water. Then a small platform breaks clear. It stops, dripping mud, and hovers just above the lake's surface. The buru leaps onto it and beckons. Against my better judgement, I follow.

***

The facility looks even more decrepit up close. The travelling platform halts outside the largest hole. The small, white, human face resolves into that of a young girl—well almost. She looks human except for yellow eyes and a dusting of rainbow coloured feathers where her eyebrows should have been.

'Dinuth!' cries the girl and launches herself to embrace the alien's leg.

The buru places a large hand on her golden hair. 'Well met, Jane. But we have guests who are injured. Run. Tell the others to prepare the vaccine chamber.'

Jane peeks around the alien's muscled leg. 'You're lucky he found you, you know.' Then she smiles. 'Don't look so afraid. You're safe here.'

***

The vaccine chamber is the one place so far on the ship that looks cared for. Rusted gantries and ruined quarters lined the journey to this room, but here the metal surfaces look newly made, gleaming like ice under the glare of acid white lights.

Dinuth places Soleil on a steel bench. He adjusts her wings and legs to rest comfortably and then reaches for a tube tied to a frame above. He inserts its needle-end into her foreleg. My sister doesn't move. I fear she is already dead.

He presses a button on a panel below the bench. Thick purple liquid courses down the clear tube and into my sister's leg. She takes a deep breath and then settles back. The alien's shoulders slump and his head bows for a moment.

'We made it. Your sister will live.' He sounds weary.

'What are you putting in her?'

Dinuth looks up. 'Viperion vaccine.' He straightens. 'I am a chemist. I have developed vaccines for most venoms from reptile-human mutations.'

'Why would you do that?'

'I developed them while trying to perfect the process for my other work.'

Uneasy, I swallow. 'What other work?'

'I can show you.'

I glance at Soleil.

'Your sister will remain asleep for a short while. We will return before she wakes.'

I don't want to leave her, but the need to have questions answered presses more urgently. I nod and Dinuth heads for the door.

Dim light filters down through the ragged holes in the hull to light the gantries. They crisscross the vaulted, cavernous space within the ship like tendons through a body. As we move deeper, the structures seem to be in better repair. But the stink of the lake lingers, a pervasive stench. Dinuth's boots clang against the metal grates. The light grows dimmer still as we move down another level. The black, oily-looking lake ripples far below. Gently swelling, its surface catches light in places it shouldn't. I'll bet death lingers in that water. This ship is as good as a tomb.

The gantry ends at an access hatch. The use of many hands has worn rust off the handle. Dinuth pushes on it and the door creaks open. Inside is a balcony and staircase that looks over a room filled with white electric light and laughter.

Dinuth moves to one side as I step across the threshold. I stare in wonder at the group of human children clustered around a table. They are eating food I haven't seen in many long years. The scents of garlic and warm bread make my mouth water—roasted mushrooms and lemon juice over warm, steaming fish.

How can there be humans here? I count at least ten in all. I glance back at Dinuth, lost for words. His lip quirks up, his blood-red eyes suddenly don't seem so terrifying.

He holds a hand out over the scene. 'My work,' he says. 'A cure for mutation.'

My sister's face flashes before me.

'You can change mutants back?' I whisper the words, afraid their truth is so fragile as to fade away.

'Well, almost,' says Dinuth. 'The process has not been perfected. I am as yet unable to split away all the genetic modifications, but they are as close to human as they can get.'

I spot Jane at a far table. Her feathered brow glistens in the light. She seems human enough for the small addition not to matter.

'Why?' I ask. 'Why would you mutate us if you mean to change us back?'

'I do not represent buru interests,' says Dinuth. 'In their opinion, I would be considered a traitor.'

My eyes narrow. I consider his admission—try to work his angle. Why would he want these human children? Why would he collect them here? Is he trying to create a child army to draw out the last vestiges of humanity still resisting his kind?

Dinuth must sense my hesitation. 'These children are here because it is not safe for them to reside outside. They would be captured again and the other buru would discover my work. They would come for me and destroy everything.'

'Why do you care about humans?'

Dinuth tilts his chin. 'I was not always buru,' he says. 'I came from another place—a peaceful world— also invaded by them. All my people were mutated into hybrid creatures—made into mindless warriors. I alone was permitted to keep my free mind because of my knowledge of chemical compounds. I could help the buru create new crossbreed species—make stronger soldiers for their armies. But to control me, they changed me—mutated me into their image.' He grabs his own chin. 'This is not the face I was born with. I know what it is too lose yourself, to have your essence corrupted.' His gaze grows distant. 'So, I learnt their methods. I perfected the science. And then I escaped. Now I work to at least give your kind back their identity. I wish to save humanity.'

And I believe him. I'm not sure why, but I do. I've killed a hundred buru in my quest to save my sister. Looked into those hundred pairs of eyes as the light faded from them. Never once have I seen the torment I now see in Dinuth's gaze.

I glance back at the groups of children laughing below. 'And you can do this for my sister? You can change her back.'

Dinuth nods. 'I already have. I added the modifier to the vaccine. Your sister will be herself when you return.'

My chest squeezes and my eyes burn with tears I have held back for ten years. My sister. I'll finally be able to tell her that I am sorry.

***

An explosion rocks the ruined vessel. The hull groans and a rain of rust, debris, and embers falls from the tattered hull. We collapse to the gantry, choking on the filthy air.

I cough. 'What the hell was that?'

'Buru weaponry,' says Dinuth. 'Missile by the sound of it. How did they find me?'

'I told you they were coming!'

The muscles in the alien's cheeks bunch. He knows as well as I do that it doesn't matter how they got here. We just need to get out.

Dinuth stands. 'They'll send in their mutants next. We need to get to the weapons store.'

'How far away is that?'

He points to the roof. 'Maybe too far.'

I look up. Dusk's red glow filters through the holes in the hull. Then the light disappears as a wave of shadows flood across. Shapes shift and blur. A horde of mutated bodies—an army—coming to snuff out the spark of hope that Dinuth has built here.

He places an urgent hand on my shoulder and squeezes. 'Please. Go back and protect the children. I'll get your sister and additional weapons. We will make our stand in the common room.'

I hesitate, unsure. Do I get my sister and run or stand and fight with this buru traitor?

'Surely you trust me by now?' asks Dinuth.

'Okay.' I pull out my xiphos and hand it to him. He takes it, wide-eyed.

'I'll give you five minutes,' I say, 'then I'm coming to get my blade back off you.'

Dinuth's smile is grim. He nods and turns, gone before I even know he's left.

***

The children are huddled under tables pulled together in a type of fort. The younger ones are crying, salt tears falling down their smooth, pink cheeks. The older children stand ready with makeshift weapons— pots and kitchen knives. They tense as I enter.

'I'm here to help.' I move forward, but the children are wary.

'Who are you?' calls an older boy with slit-pupilled eyes like a lizard's.

Jane crawls out from under a table. Her hair has fallen free of its ponytail. 'She's with Dinuth,' she says to the boy. 'She's got a sister here being changed back. We can trust her.'

The boy's eyes narrow but then he nods. He hands me his kitchen knife.

I reach back and pull my shotgun free. I tap my belt and the eighteen cartridges stored there.

'Thanks, but I've got my own weapon.'

The younger children quieten, and the room falls silent but for the sound of breathing. Outside, mutants roam, claws clicking over metal and raucous voices screaming in languages that have nothing to do with being human.

The seconds pass. One minute turns to four. The tearing of metal screeches out closer than before; sounds like the hull is being sheared open.

Five minutes. Still no Dinuth.

I rack my mind, trying to recall other buru ships I infiltrated in the past. My gaze slews to the far workbenches that serve here as the kitchen. The eyehooks welded into the surfaces are something I have seen before—human bonding rooms.

There are large drainage ducts below those benches.

'Quickly, children,' I whisper as the noises outside the room grow louder. 'To the benches.' I sprint the fifteen metres and drop to the ground. I take the knife off the boy and wedge the tip into the metal plate flooring. A grated panel slides free to reveal a dark passage below.

'Get in here,' I say to the huddled children. 'These ducts will conceal you while I go to find Dinuth. Crawl down as far as you can.' I hand the knife back to the boy. 'When you reach water, start prying at the side panels. They'll open to the hull's skin. Swim for the forest.'

'But there are monsters there,' whimpers Jane.

'There are more monsters here,' I say. 'You have a better chance of survival hidden in the trees.'

I look to the older boy. 'Get them across the lake and into the forest. Head north until you find the corpse of a female snake mutant. Go about sixty metres further on into the undergrowth. Behind the wild ginger clump there's a hatch to an underground bunker—my home. Hide there and we will come for you.'

The boy nods and disappears into the duct. The others follow.

Only Jane hesitates. 'Promise you will come for us?'

A smile is all I have to comfort her. 'I promise,' I say.

She disappears into the hole. I replace the plate and stand. Time to find Dinuth and my sister.

****

The ruined ship crawls with mutants. Viperions, griffinous, and others I cannot name, but all equally terrifying. I cling to the shadows easing my way along the gantry towards Soleil's room. My gun is loaded and ready to fire.

Ahead, a commotion. A group of humanoid insects by the look of their diaphanous wings, faceted eyes and black exoskeletons. They batter at a door with a rusty beam, chittering and cackling as the door shudders with each hit. Something in there has drawn their attention. It can only be one thing.

I aim and fire. The first shots plough into the mutants. Some fall and others flit away to hover in the darkness. I reload, the pump action sliding smoothly. I fire again, surging ahead. My back meets the damaged door. I yell out.

'It's me. Let me in!'

The door creaks open and Dinuth pulls me through. The metal panel slams shut and the hatch is sealed.

'Where are the children?' he snarls. His armour is scratched and mired with blood. The fight to this room doesn't seem to have been easy.

'Getting off this ship.'

'You have as good as murdered them!'

'No,' I growl back. 'I gave them a chance to live. We'll die if we stay here.'

Dinuth swings away. A vial of vaccine glistens purple at his belt. He scowls but what can he do?

The battering outside starts again.

Dinuth turns back, face resolute. He steps to one side.

But I barely see him.

Because *she* is standing just behind him, dressed in buru armour and with my xiphos held tightly in her right hand.

Soleil.

Tall, blonde and eyes like a summer sky.

My sister is human again.

Almost.

At her throat, she wears a collar of pure white feathers.

'Aster?' Her voice is a whisper, as if she has forgotten how to speak our language.

'Oh god,' I sob. Tears brim over and my throat feels dry. So many things to say but the hammering outside grows more insistent.

Not nearly enough time to say it all.

So, I holster my gun and run to her.

She feels bird-like and feather light in the circle of my arms.

'It's okay,' she whispers into my ear. 'I know and I love you, too.'

But no time to linger. I pull back and smile at her. 'Ready to hunt?'

She nods, grinning, and together, we turn to face the door.

Soleil wields the blade. I hold the shotgun. Dinuth, unable to secure other weapons, has only his blaster but, as old as it is, I doubt it's worth the metal it's made from.

The door buckles. Another hit and it skews sideways, ragged lock left hanging. The insects outside see us through the gap. They grow agitated. Claws rake at the opening, wings clatter and batter like panels of fragile plastic against the door pillar.

'Hold steady,' whispers Dinuth.

I can almost taste his fear—it has the same flavour as my own. Beside me, Soleil shifts and gulps. She has never fought anyone while in human form. But her jaw hardens and her grip on the weapon is steady.

The door falls inwards and the mutants heave forward. Black carapaces glint in the light and razor claws scrabble across the panelled metal floor. The room fills with their inhuman voices and the stench of their carrion-laced breaths.

Dinuth moves first. His blaster sizzles a bolt of energy into the foremost insectoid. It falls into a pile of smoking ash. The others crawl over it—uncaring. Dinuth fires again, but this time the blaster fails, the old tech ruined by neglect.

I step into the breach. The shotgun roars and more mutants fall, their gore splattering the floor. But it's not enough. Soleil dances into the fight, light-footed and quick. Wielding the xiphos in one hand, she carves it into the wall of thick, brittle chitin. The blade glimmers, an arc of polished steel. Wing fragments fly, floating like pearlescent glitter. Black blood follows, splattering her face and the wall and the floor.

Dinuth uses the blaster like a club. A mutant ducks past his defences and plunges its razor-tipped claws through a gap in his armour. Between the hip and the abdomen. Dinuth grunts and punches the creature in the face. It falls backwards, and so does he.

Overwhelmed by the numbers, I fire round after round. The chamber clicks empty. My last nine rounds are loaded. My empty ammo belt feels too light for comfort. I shoot again.

The gun jams.

'Shit, not again,' I snarl, working to clear the breach. It frees. I snap the gun back to my shoulder and squeeze the trigger. The recoil is a bitch when this time it fires.

Bodies pile up against the opening. One shot. Two. More shots. Then nothing moves in the doorway. It's blocked. The other mutants can't get through. I glance down. Still got two bullets left.

Soleil, splattered with black blood and xiphos in hand, stands breathless by the door. 'Is he okay?' she asks, eyes on Dinuth.

I kneel by the buru. His hand flutters by his belt. The vial. But it lies shattered at his side, purple liquid scattered across the ground.

His fingers touch the fluid and his breath catches. His eyes close. 'It's gone,' he says. 'Everything I worked for. Lost. The buru have won.'

But I'm not willing to let these goddamned aliens win.

'Not yet they haven't.' I tear a strip of fabric from the hem of my shirt and plug his wound. 'Here hold this,' I say.

Dinuth presses his palm to the wad. 'What are you doing?'

'Getting us the hell out of here.'

'But the formula is gone.'

I lean in close to his face. 'But you aren't. You created it before and you can do it again. And maybe, just maybe, you can perfect it with the help of me and Soleil. Maybe our DNA is the answer. One was mutated, one not. That's what you need, isn't it? A comparison?'

Dinuth's eyes widen.

'Now, I'm going to get us all out of here,' I say. 'We get the kids and we set up a new lab in my bunker.'

'And get back to work,' whispers Dinuth.

'Exactly. We have aliens to destroy and humanity to save.'

I turn to my sister. 'Hand me that blade.'

She nods and takes my shotgun. Her gaze catches mine. She smiles. My heart squeezes again. It's so good to have her back.

Then I press the tip of the xiphos to the metal plate in the floor.

It lifts.

The darkness of the duct beneath beckons.

THREE DOOR SALOON

Jack

I have one chance in three to secure my heart's desire. But choose wrong and I'll either be frozen in a cryotube or sent to Hell via a swing from the gallows tree.

The Long Sleep, or The Long Death.

I go in knowing the odds. Just as my older sister and my father both did before me. One in three and I'm the third.

The outcome has to fall in my favour, right?

My father's corpse hangs bloating in the heat. The shoelace, loosened from his boot, dangles limp in the empty space beneath his feet. Bones litter the ground under him. I turn away from the dry breeze that carries the stench of his death to me and ignore the creak of the hanging rope as his body shifts.

A memory from three nights ago, of us both huddled over our campfire, returns to me.

'Now, son,' said my father. 'The demon keeps the colours of the doors a secret. We can only guess at what your sister picked, but either way I'll choose the darkest colour. That'll cut the odds for you' His eyes glitter in the firelight. 'If we both choose wrong— then we go to Plan B.'

'You sure there's no other way to do this, Pa? I ain't got a good feelin' about it.'

'Look, Jack. I made my peace with dyin' a while back. Ever since I found out I was sick. Your sister should never have gone to that place to try an' save me.' He'd pointed to his stomach and the cancerous tumours hidden within it. 'I'm a dead man anyhow. And I'll be damned if your sister will be left to rot forever in a cryotube on account of me, do you understand? We get her back. No matter the cost.'

No matter the cost.

The recollections of firelight and my father fade, replaced by the reality of a dusty street leading into the even dustier town of Esperance. The town is a two-bit hovel clinging to the edge of the prairie—the arse end of the West. But what I've come for can only be found here. The Three Door Saloon huddled at the far end of Main Street.

My palm settles on the butt of the pistol holstered at my side—the pistol I use as a lawman to protect people and property. It's tempting to go in, all guns blazing, and usually I would, but this time gunpowder won't solve my problems. This time it'll need to be brains over brawn.

And I've got plenty of both to choose from.

I unpin my badge of office and pocket it. I rub my hands down the front of my vest and adjust my hat.

Time to get the job done.

***

The saloon doors hang limp from their hinges, rough and weathered as the posts holding up the sagging porch roof. I hesitate. The reality I've been ignoring suddenly hits me. It's all distilled to this. The fate of my entire family rides on my father's horse-shit crazy plan.

The doors give way to my hand, swinging open with a squeal. Odours roll past me—whiskey and tobacco smoke. It's bright inside, sunlight filtering in through the windowpanes and painting shadows across the worn floor. While not a plush establishment, it's well presented. Somehow, I expected something more sinister. But no. Dolo the Rogue Trader's saloon is full of light. An unexpected backdrop for a man who deals in souls, wishes, and death.

I step across the threshold and into the room proper. All eyes turn. Except Dolo's. Dressed in a charcoal, pinstriped suit, he sits dealing cards to two others at the poker table—a man and a finely-dressed woman. I suppose it doesn't matter to him who walks through those doors. Only that they do. *Come in, come in, little chickens*, he must think. *I love a good game of chance.*

***

<u>*Dolo*</u>

The man enters, a youngish gunslinger, but built big. At six foot tall he looks more like a bull-rider than a gunman. Pistols hang low on his hips. His eyes, dark as coal, glare from under the brim of his ten-gallon hat. His glance slews across the room, falling first on the barman, who continues to polish the whiskey glasses, then past the poker table and the working girls lounging by the staircase. His gaze falls on The Wall.

The Wall. My personal gallery of victories. The display of cryotubes, stacked vertically twenty wide and ten high, is where I store the catatonic. Well—I let them rest there until I'm desperate and running low on souls to send to Hell.

The man's gaze falls on the young red-headed girl in the highest tube. She came in last month to try her hand at the Three Doors.

The gunslinger's full red beard twitches as he considers the face of the woman. I grin. So he has come for the girl. Just like the old man did yesterday. Could this be another family member perhaps? A brother?

How delightful. Snaring that one little woman has proven quite profitable. Because of her, I'll have three strong souls tallied these last few months alone. I flick another card out onto the table. But my interest in poker has passed. Now I'm intent on a different game. I nod to Wyatt, the barman. He's one of the lower demons in my employ and has the good fortune to almost look human, except for his slitted pupils.

He places the glass he is polishing down on the countertop. 'Mornin',' he says to the gunslinger. 'You here for the whiskey or the doors?'

Red-beard's fingers twitch, like he's uncomfortable without guns in his fist. I've seen his type before. All brawn but no brains.

Red-beard tips his chin towards The Wall. 'I'm here for what those folk all came for.'

Wyatt glances over at me. I smile, long and slow. I tap my unlooked-at cards into a stack and place them neatly onto the table. My heels rock the chair back to rest on its rear legs. 'Well then, shall we be gettin' started?'

Red-Beard's gaze bores into me. Something in his eyes unsettles me. A kind of resolve I've not seen before. Most people come here with hope. But this man?

A chill coils down my spine.

My chair legs hit the floor again with a crack. I rise, focussing on the theatrics of my game to settle my unease. 'Everyone out,' I say. My gaze shifts to Red-Beard. 'Except you.'

With a grating of chairs and the rustle of fabrics, the patrons in the saloon leave. When all is quiet, I saunter to the wall opposite the cryotube display. A heavy, red velvet curtain, its hem puddling on the floor like new spilled blood, conceals what's behind. Red-Beard's eyes burn as he watches me draw it across.

And the reason why the Three Door Saloon is named such is revealed.

Three doors fitted in the wall.

Red, white, and black.

***

Jack

The room is silent—empty—except for Dolo, his wall of collected souls and me. When the doors in the wall are revealed, those stored in the cryotubes behind me stir.

Horrified, I watch them awaken, dazed, from their frozen sleep. It takes only a moment for them to recall where they are. Their movements grow with sudden urgency. They claw at their glass prisons, screaming silently at me—perhaps telling me the cost is not worth the gain. But I can't hear them through the barrier. I falter when my gaze falls on my sister. Josie. She kneels in her tube, tears tracking down her cheeks. Desperately, she points to her dress. Over and over. Her lips move. I can't be sure what she's saying, but imagine I know—*Not you too.*

My father's last words echo in my mind.

No matter the cost.

It's like pulling teeth to turn away from her. But I do it, determined to see this through.

The three doors almost fill the wall. Built from simple timber slats braced across with two rusted iron belts, they seem unassuming. But I don't make the mistake of thinking that doesn't mean deadly. I rub my hand down my face and tug on my beard. The room suddenly feels hot. Sweat drips off my forehead.

I glance at Dolo. 'So how does this work?'

Dolo smiles. His teeth sharp and impossibly white. A glint of red flickers behind his green eyes and the stories I've heard about him suddenly seem like they might be true.

Demon.

Devil.

Murderer.

My hard-won resolve wavers. I re-focus on my father and Josie. I grit my teeth. 'Do I just choose?' I ask.

'First,' says Dolo. 'You need to tell me what you want.'

I glare at him. 'You know damn well why I'm here. I want my sister back.'

Dolo tilts his head. Light splinters off his oiled hair and a diamond stud pressed into his ear lobe. 'What is your name, boy?' he asks. 'You remind me of someone I recently met.'

'I'm Jack,' I growl.

'Jack,' says Dolo as if the word provides illumination. 'You would be Jack Junior then. You look a lot like the man who came to us yesterday.'

'Aye. That man was my father.'

'Such a shame he died.' Dolo frowns but he doesn't truly look sad. 'You know you can't save them both today? If you win, one wish can only buy you one life.'

I'd heard the rules were such from the townsfolk. I shrug and let words, carefully rehearsed, fall from my lying lips. 'I hated my father. He was a bastard. He hurt all manner of folk in his day. If he's in Hell, that's where he deserves to be.'

Dolo's eyes narrow. His fine, long fingers tap a slow tattoo on his chest. 'All right then. It's a deal. Your sister or your soul. Choose your door, Jack Junior. The odds are one in three to win.'

My father chose the darkest.

So only two options remain. I recall my sister pointing to her dress. I glance back at her strained face. Her hand clutches at the sleeve of her blouse. Her favourite white dress. Was she suggesting she chose the white door? Yes. That must be it. I make my choice.

'Red for the win,' I say.

Dolo frowns again and for a moment my heart surges. I've won—this nightmare is over! But then comes his wicked smile and my heart sinks into my boots.

'Wrong,' he says. 'Red is for Hell. And that is your destination. What a good son you are to follow in your father's footsteps.'

Dolo's hand flicks up. Red electricity trips across his palm. It crackles outward towards the doors, colliding with and shattering them into a thousand splinters.

The doors and the wall of the saloon are gone. A new, ragged-edged hole has opened, looking out over a burning landscape. This isn't the township of Esperance. I'm beholding Hell.

I grit my teeth, grinding back the rage that urges me to the stupidity of pulling my guns. The red door was the right answer. I'm sure of it. Dolo's a liar. His game must be rigged.

Plan B it is.

I only hope my father was right in his assumptions.

The rocky plain of brimstone glows against a stygian infinity. The stench of sulphur catches in my throat. I cough but can't clear it.

A black chain appears, hanging coiled from Dolo's fist. 'Usually, you would be set for the gallows tree,' he says. 'But it has been a busy month for business. The rules say your father's corpse must occupy that spot until his bones fall.' He smiles a smile, a thin, cruel thing filled with malice. 'So,' he says. 'Today you receive a special honour. I shall escort you to Hell, myself.'

'Honestly, it's okay,' I say. 'If you're busy an' all, I can be comin' back some other time.'

'Not at all,' says Dolo. 'It will be my pleasure.' He strides forward. He flicks his wrist and the chain, both searing hot and freezing cold, falls to coil around my wrists.

***

Dolo

It's been an age since I was last forced to walk through Hell. It is a decidedly less pleasant place than the human world. The air tastes rank—of bone-smoke and ash. And the cries of the damned are an irritating background litany.

I lead the gunslinger towards the Binding Fields. Past rugged piles of charred rock and the shattered bones of a thousand beings, they finally emerge. A wretched stretch of barren soil dotted with the petrified skeletons of long-dead trees. To each of these is tied a hanged soul—souls that I sent here. They are the coin I give to the Burning One in exchange for my freedom to roam Earth. Hundreds swing here, all victims fallen to the promise of my charmed doors.

I tug the gunslinger closer. He stumbles, his boots catching on an edge of old bone peeking out of the dirt. His breaths are irregular; the fumes not suitable to sustain human lungs. No matter. He won't have a need to breathe for much longer.

We pass the first trees. A woman hangs there, her shadowy face filled with anguish. 'My baby,' she sighs in a voice tired and thin. 'I just wanted him back.'

How these pathetic souls disgust me. All wishing and wanting.

The next is an older man, his sightless eyes rolling in their sockets. 'Can I choose another door?' he asks plaintively. 'I just want to see again.'

The gunslinger pulls against the chain and stops walking. His eyes look like bruises in the dim light. 'All these people. What does their pain buy you?' he asks, his voice scuffed raw by the atmosphere.

I jerk on the chain, but the boy pulls back. Even weakened by this place, he is still strong. I decide it's better to answer him. 'What everyone wants,' I say. 'Freedom.'

'No man is truly free,' mutters the boy.

The mortal dares judge me? What he doesn't understand is that their frail little lives are the currency of the supernatural. They are nothing more than oil to line the cogs of eternity.

I growl and lean in closer. 'Then it's lucky I am no man.'

I pull harder on the chain this time and the gunslinger falls to one knee. 'Get up,' I snarl. 'And don't speak again.'

The gunslinger glares at me but holds his tongue. He pushes upright, awkwardly. I lead him onward, draw him on to the next empty tree. He's annoyed me now, so I'll make sure his eternity is all the harder to bear. I'll take him to hang next to the father he hates—next to Jack Senior. For to have his soul to despair a little more is not a bad thing anyway. Any hope in his heart and the armies of Heaven will sense him and descend to take him away. And a lost soul means my freedom could be revoked.

The tree next to Jack's father is a shattered thing. Broken like the souls that surround it. Its skeleton glows scarlet in the light of distant hell-fires. I wrench on the chain again. The gunslinger pulls back again. Irritated, I clench my jaw and turn but his eyes are not on me. They are locked on his father.

The older man is looking at the sky. His eyes are trained on the empty black and his lips move. 'No matter the cost. No matter the cost.'

'Dad?' whispers the gunslinger.

The father stops muttering. His eyes swivel down.

'Hello, Jacky,' he says. 'Plan B then?'

'Aye,' whispers the son.

***

Jack

My heart twists seeing my father on that tree.

But it was what we planned—what needed to happen if he didn't win his turn at Dolo's doors.

My father smiles. 'So the game *is* rigged!' he whispers. 'The game is rigged!'

The other souls on the trees around us start to chant also. 'The game is rigged. The game is rigged.'

Dolo snarls. He tugs me forward and this time I comply. I step up to the tree he has chosen for me. He loops the loose length of the chain around my neck and throws the rest over the closest tree branch. He leans down to pick up the end—

I strike.

With all my force I knee Dolo in the chin. His head snaps back but he doesn't fall. Slowly, steadily he stands up, turns and looks at me. His oiled hair, fallen free, hangs like fat leeches over his forehead. His eyes narrow and his lips press into thin white lines. 'You done now, Jack Junior?' he says.

I flex my fingers, wishing my wrists were free. 'Not even nearly,' I say.

Faster than my eye can follow, Dolo yanks the chain taut and hauls me into the air. The black links bite into the soft flesh of my throat. My spine slams against the iron-hard tree at my back.

But my neck doesn't break.

It's to be a slow death.

Around me, voices rise—angry. 'The game is rigged!' they cry. 'The game is rigged!'

Dolo wrenches the chain again. It tightens further. My vision darkens. I fall limp.

Maybe Plan B won't work after all.

Is the game rigged?

But then the chain loosens and I drop an inch. I swivel my gaze to Dolo. He's pale and struggling to hold my weight. He staggers forward. I drop another inch. Then the hanged souls nearby remove their nooses and crawl down from their trees. They move like shadows in the wind, one moment solid, the next opaque. They gather. They gather. They surround Dolo. The chain slips from his grip, and I slither down to land on my feet. The Rogue Trader's chest heaves. His eyes glow a dull red. Malicious. Malevolent.

I unwind the chain off my neck and draw in a foul-tasting breath. Breathing never felt so good. Then, of their own accord, the bindings on my wrists fall away. I stand with my hands on my knees for a moment, eyes closed.

A hand squeezes my shoulder.

I look up. My father. 'You did it, son,' he says. 'Look.' He points. 'The Burning One comes.'

A fiery figure stalks the horizon. It draws closer, its shape solidifying into a man with eyes like two coals and a body of flame. A darkly burning phoenix rides his shoulder.

The souls surrounding us part, stepping aside. Dolo cringes as he lays eyes on the being. 'My Lord. Why have you come?' he says.

The Burning One tilts his chin. 'These souls have found hope, Dolo.' He raises his arms to encompass the crowd of gathered souls. 'You took three from the same family and now they believe your game is a cheat. They no longer despair.'

Dolo's face twists. He points to the crowd. 'I didn't cheat anyone. You all accepted the odds—one chance in three—and lost. Back to your trees.'

'No,' says the Burning One. He looks up as the black sky arching overhead fractures into glowing lines of white. 'It is too late. The Heavenly Others already come to claim them.'

Dolo blanches. 'But the game doesn't work like that.'

'Your game was never about the odds, Dolo. It was about giving me despairing souls in return for your freedom,' says the Burning One. 'And now, the belief of your victims, right or wrong, holds power. You took the son, the third of his family-line for you to claim. He believed you cheated him for he was confident he chose the right door. Then you brought him across the threshold with a heart full of hope. That was your mistake, Dolo.'

'This is unfair.'

'No. You played your own game and lost.' The Burning One's chin tilts up. 'And now all the souls you gathered for me are lost. Our deal is broken. You will return to Hell and remain here.'

'Please,' stutters Dolo. 'Wait…'

But the trader's words fall on deaf ears. The dark phoenix rises off the Burning One's shoulders. Where it flies, embers fall from the tips of its wings. It circles Dolo and he begins to change. His human features shift to become monstrous—long-fanged and red-eyed. His arms grow into legs and he becomes dog-like in form. Then he howls, an inhuman call that echoes off the plain, and runs, disappearing into the distance.

Then the sky tears apart. The Heavenly Others. Sunlight falls on the ruined plains and a gentle breeze starts to blow. I look around. Every soul faces the light, beatific smiles painted on their broken lips. Next to me, my father sighs. 'I'm proud of you, Jack,' he says. 'You did it.'

'We did it,' I reply.

Heat touches my left side. The Burning One approaches, the phoenix returned to his shoulder. 'I will grant you the one wish Dolo should have given you,' he says. 'Choose, human.'

My father smiles at me. 'It's okay,' he says. 'It's gotta be Josie. It's high time I be movin' on in any case. I'm happy to go.'

I'll miss my father but know it's what he really wants. I embrace him then turn to the Burning One. 'I'll take a good life, sir,' I say. 'With my sister in it.'

The Burning One frowns. 'One wish for one soul. You and your sister are both mine. You may save yourself or your sister, but I cannot grant both. Choose again.'

My father stalks past me and stares down the Burning Man. 'The game was rigged. Jack doesn't belong to you.'

'I am truly sorry,' says the Burning One. 'But your son perished the moment he stepped across the door's threshold into my domain. He is mine. The rules are clear.'

My father's face twists. He turns to me. 'I'm so sorry, Jacky. I got it wrong.'

I frown. My father has only ever tried to do his best for us kids. Now it's my turn to step up and do what's best for him. Time to protect my own. 'Nah. It's all right, Pa, we got it right. This is just the cost.'

Before my father can say anything else, I lift my chin and stare the Burning One in the eye. 'I choose freedom for my sister.'

The Burning One bows.

The phoenix launches.

Embers rain down.

The last thing I see, framed by the light of the Heavenly Others' arrival, is the main street of Esperance.

And my sister on the porch, in her white dress, gaze searching.

LEGACY OF THE SPECIES

When the alien archaeologists come—and it is my hope they will come—first they will see the worst of what humanity wreaked upon our planet. They will note the broken-backed cities, the endless oceans of sand dotted with ancient bones, and ash-grey skies that weep black tears over it all. But then, once they sift through all the debris and the old blood, they will discover Repository; the last bastion of beauty on this planet.

My father told me that the story of humanity began in the Garden of Eden so it makes sense, in a certain ironic kind of way, that it ends here also. Eden is no longer a terrestrial paradise. The once fertile garden lies ruined by the fallout of a worldwide war, diminished into a shallow cradle of red earth and limp plants. Dead trees clutch the sky and implore, 'Please don't let it end like this. Humanity showed such promise.'

Even the serpent's skeleton, coiled in the almost-dead branches of Adam's apple tree seems to have an opinion on the matter, albeit a different one.

'Humanity. You've done Hell proud.'

I can't say I disagree with him.

But still, there are parts of us worth saving.

I wipe the back of my hand across my brow. Sand particles cling to the sweat like magnets. Moisture means life, and in this place even the dirt fears death. I glance at the forty-nine timber crosses erected along the garden wall—the resting places of my neighbours and family. All who came to this last safe place in the days before the nuclear missiles fell are gone now. I am alone and the weight of that loneliness presses on me.

I shuffle the three apple-sized rocks that sit heavy in the cradle of my elbow. The baetylus, mined from the fallen arch of Eden's jade gates, are stones that ancient mythology claims were endowed with life by the gods. Or so, again, my father told me. But, as a scientist from back before the world fell, I know the truth. They are meteorites, heavy in composition with the silver-white metal palladium—a metal that, when properly manipulated, has the ability to recall and represent memory.

Ahead, Repository beckons. The tall, windowless tower is built from blocks of black stone fallen from the Garden's formidable walls. The door stands open leading into darkness. Its smooth, circular lines promise sanctuary from the heat and watery grey light.

I squint up at the endless stretch of grim sky. The sun's pale, sickly sphere glares through the ash cloud.

'Hurry! Hurry! Mortal,' he seems to whisper. 'Time's bowstring is taut. Her arrow is aimed. This moment is the pause before the release.'

Time.

Time has been fair to me for the last twenty years; she has sustained me. But now, with the garden's meagre produce failing, her influence has run its course. I lick my lips, dry and cracked. No use in pondering what is lost. I head for the doorway, faded linen robes raising dust and sandals scuffing the well-worn path.

Cold air floods out from within. The gentle purr of a generator whirring in the building's depths tells me the atmospheric filters are still running. I step through and into the precisely cylindrical room, fifty metres in diameter. Dark, polished walls encircle me. A plaque carved in white granite and gold stands on a plinth in the centre.

The Repository of Humanity
To be human was art.
Both good and ill.
Judge us not on our failures alone,
But by the beauty that defined us also.

My mother's words. In contrast to the scientific pursuits of my father, grandfather, and myself, she considered herself a seer. My mother knew best our spiritual nature, believing humans could be many things: devils and angels, architects and demolitionists.

Even saviours.

I climb a short staircase and enter the next level of the tower. The Gallery. Fifty plinths of black stone rise from the floor, arrayed in concentric circles. On forty-six rest activated baetylus, each set into a cradle that connects them to the underground geothermic power grid my grandfather built before he died.

A collaboration of science and god-stones.

I press my fingers to the closest baetyl. It rises out of the cradle and shivers. The palladium, adjusted by my isotope treatment process, splits into a cloud of particles and hovers, contained, like a swarm of microscopic bees. The ball tightens and liquefies, forming into a floating sphere of mercurial fluid. Colour rolls across the surface, a wash of watercolour hues. The flux stabilises and a flat plane solidifies. It spins gently above the plinth, held aloft by the cradle's energy field.

A picture frame.

An image.

The Mona Lisa.

Her smile is as enigmatic as ever. Her metallic cheek ripples gently as I brush it. Leonardo da Vinci's masterpiece is held preserved within the stone. This was the memory my brother donated to our cause. Always a fan of the older works. I miss him and our conversations. My hand drops. Mona Lisa remains for a moment longer then she folds away like origami as the meteorite's true shape reasserts dominance. The baetyl settles gently back down into its cradle.

It is only a fleeting vision, a limitation of the technology.

But this was the only method I could devise to preserve the works.

I cross the room and pass the largest plinth of all. The fiftieth. At two metres square, it dominates the space. Its cradle waits empty, claws open like a lotus flower's petals. This one I have reserved for the largest baetyl stone—one I mined long ago—the keystone of the gate's arch.

I don't look as I pass it by.

My small workshop, located on the third level, is a low-ceilinged room with a small hearth, bed and two pitchers filled with the last of my precious water.

I enter to warm, yellow electric light and the scent of mechanical things. A table lines one wall. Its scarred surface holds glass vessels, old computer screens and the last synaptic chips in existence.

The chips. The technology used to control the baetylus. They are also my key to Hell—and I will go to Hell—because I designed them. Even as I discovered how to attach memory engrams to the chip's base programs, I knew the dire cost.

I knew what it meant to use them on humans.

But I called the people to me anyway. I asked them to donate the best of themselves; convinced them that the sacrifice of doing so was worth the cost. Then I connected the chips to their skulls and rifled and pillaged and stole what they remembered. I stored their personal visions of art; I took their joy.

And watched every single one of them die as I did it.

Am I a murderer?

What choice did I have?

The reader waits for me on the table, red lights blinking on its LED interface. I choose a synaptic chip and insert it into the access port. I lean into the viewfinder.

A book. But not fiction like others already recorded in several baetylus in the gallery. This one is precious. A grandmother's recipe book. I press the shift button on the reader and the pages flip. Recipe follows recipe, handwritten in the cursive style that belonged to a long-gone era—an era before computers and the fallout of nuclear weapons. A simpler life. A simpler time. I bite back tears as the recipes blur past. Apple and Rhubarb Pie. Spaghetti Bolognaise. Christmas Fruit Cake.

I was twenty when Earth's last Christmas was celebrated.

Where have the last two decades gone?

I remove the chip from the reader and look for the name printed on the back.

Anne McLain - 12th June 2080.

Anne was my grandmother's best friend. I remember her soft voice as I connected her to the chip. She was nervous, but resolute. But the oldest people were all the same—spines of steel. She'd gritted her teeth as the pressure built in her skull. The chip then siphoned the recollection of her grandmother's cooking. The art of the chef.

'Her legacy is safe, Anne,' I whisper.

A bowl of synaptic fluid sits next to the reader. The baetyl I choose slips in quietly, its pale matrix softening in the liquid. I press the chip to the meteorite. It accepts the offering, absorbing it. The stone's form flutters uncertainly in response to the unfamiliar technology. Once fused, the chip is integral, acting as a brain of sorts.

But one further small sacrifice is needed to make the memory stick.

I prick my finger and a bead of blood wells up. I lift the stone and smear the blood across its surface— a drop of my life for the memory to live. The baetyl's shape shifts. In moments, Anne's recipe book sits in my palm. I flip the delicate metallic pages, lettering inked in gold over the impervious surface. I turn and place it on the table beside me. The book folds back into the baetyl's original shape as soon as my touch releases it.

The next chip slots into the reader. Drawings fill the screen—architectural drawings. I lean in to read the strong, confident lettering.

Sydney Opera House, Australia.
Front Elevation, 1959.

I smile in delight. Gregor Utzon, descendant of the original architect, Jørn Utzon, gave this one. I savour the delicate tracery of linework and the splendid wash of colours as they play across the image. The architect took care with his perspectives and elevations. All, rendered to scale, portray a vision of soaring lines and elegant stature. Building as art. These drawings represent the advancement of humanity—our ability to create beauty in parallel to the once-grand sprawl of living nature. It's an important vision to keep.

Another drop of blood and another stone. Soon ten large pages rest before me, metallic surfaces capturing the minute detail Gregor's donation.

The final chip slides into the reader. A drawing made by a child emerges. Two stick figures painted in scarlet and green. *Mummy and me* is scrawled below the image. Alice Jones gave this memory—a gift from her daughter, Susan, the small, blonde-haired girl who died on the perilous journey to Eden. In my mind, I imagine Susan's fingers gripping tightly to a crayon, her small tongue poked out in concentration. And then those tiny hands gifting the work to her mother who may have smiled indulgently and told her what a wonderful artist she was.

Yes. It's fitting this will fill the last baetyl.

Proof that the innocence of humanity existed.

Because God knows, as do I, it doesn't anymore.

The blood on my hands attests to that.

***

The three baetylus shift and blur as I carry them down to the gallery. Book. Drawings. Art. They fall neatly into their respective cradles, almost sighing as they settle into place. Once released, the stones resolve into their natural shape. I step back from the plinths.

Bittersweet joy fills me. This is the culmination of my work. But a deep sadness follows. The last memory is now catalogued. I hadn't thought of it in my race to beat time, but now grieve knowing I will no longer sift through beautiful things.

I take a deep breath and stare at the floor. I am acutely aware of the last plinth still sitting empty behind me. Its polished black gaze presses on my shoulder blades. The room's silence almost gives voice to the block—small but deep and inexorable.

'Still one work to go,' it seems to whisper.

One work to go.

I rub my hand down my face, callused palm scraping.

Time is up.

The switch panel by the entrance door opens with a quiet click. The switches all point up. One by one, I turn them down. First the third-floor lights. The generator. The ventilator. And last, the atmospheric controls. This art needs none of these to survive.

The heat in the room rises. I walk back to the empty plinth. My reflection stares back at me from its polished surface. Grey hair, wrinkled skin that folds down from my nose to the corners of my mouth. At forty years old, I look closer to sixty. Not that any of that matters.

I reach into my satchel and pull out the last baetyl stone. The Keystone. It weighs heavy in my fist. I imagine it as the meteor it once was, traversing the dark silence of space. I wonder if dying feels the same, a slow, quiet descent into the infinite.

I grunt as I lift the baetyl into the cradle. Already treated with synaptic fluid, the metal feels pliable to my touch. The last chip slips free from my pocket. This one is blank, no memory yet recorded in it. It weighs feather light in my hand. I pause. Hesitant. I've never siphoned a memory directly through a chip and into a baetyl before. I'm not sure if it will even work.

Technically, it should.

I bite my bottom lip.

Am I ready for this?

I giggle—a macabre twitch. It's funny that I should be afraid to die. I didn't hesitate to send the others on their way.

The synaptic chip's glue is cold against my temple. I plug a thin transfer cable from it directly into the cradle's access socket and a small alarm sounds. I wince as a needle extends, first tapping my temple then piercing my skull and penetrating the hippocampus structure. My vision blurs but I find the button to activate the cradle. Its claws crackle to life with energy drawn from the underground grid. The baetyl's shape fluctuates rapidly under the direct current, molecules moving and dancing—waiting for instruction.

My heart races. Fear claws at my throat. I fight the desire to tear the chip and its needle free.

You are about to die.

You are going to Hell.

My palms grow sweaty. My fingers twitch. I can't do this. But then the voices of those buried by the garden wall fill my mind.

'Coward!' they whisper.

They made their sacrifice willingly. They knew—come Heaven or Hell—the future holds no place for humanity.

I straighten my shoulders and lift my chin. I can do this. I prick my finger on the cradle's claw and smear my blood on the baetyl. I keep my fingers pressed to the metal.

Hell, here I come.

'I am the last of my species,' I say.

My words give the baetyl shape.

A human skeleton forms.

I grit my teeth as pressure grows behind my eyes—my memory cortex is being accessed.

'We are named "Human".'

My knowledge of DNA and genetic strands catches, and the chip begins working on the baetyl. Tiny threads of silver metal grow, weaving and twisting. Organs form. Heart, lungs, eyes and brain.

Blood vessels burgeon into actuality, building intricate networks crisscrossed over and between newly developed muscles.

'And my form is the final artwork.'

Skin. It blossoms across the body—breasts, arms and thighs—like oil over water. Then follows hair, fingers and the outline of feet.

The details of my own face resolve.

I smile, taking in the lines of my copy hovering, sleep-like, above the cradle. I pluck the chip from my temple and press it into the baetyl. It disappears into the metal.

I slither to the floor and wait. The end, I know from experience, will be quick. But three seconds turn into thirty. Something isn't right. There is no kind drowsiness to lead me out of this life.

Instead my chest starts to burn. I press my hand to my heart, the beats irregular. My breath quickens. My lungs fill with razor blades.

I look up.

Even without my touch, the artwork's shape is holding. And worse, its chest is moving in rhythm to mine, rising and falling.

The chip—the direct connection—

My life has given it life?

What have I done?

I could have saved the others!

I clutch my shirt.

Pain lances across my torso—hot as Hellfire.

My heartbeat slows.

I take a deep, shuddering breath.

Death is no easy fall into darkness.

***

The artwork floats.

Air caresses the back of its arms and neck.

It opens its eyes. The light is dim, but it can see quite well.

It sits up and stretches, metal fingers creaking as they extend, eyelids clinking like tiny bells as it blinks.

It looks down.

A clawed cradle rises below it, set into the centre of a black plinth. Transparent blue energy crackles at the machine's core holding the artwork aloft.

A forest of smaller plinths spiral out into the gloom. Other cradles glimmer on the displays, illuminating the irregular-shaped metal stones they house. The edges of said stones seem to shift uneasily—like they hold secrets. The artwork wants to reach out and touch them.

But something else calls its attention. A shadow huddled at the base of the plinth. It scans the data recorded in its synaptic chip for identification.

Corpse.

It looks with interest at the cadaver's soft skin and the watery green eyes as they stare into the middle distance—so different to the artwork's own metal structure. It wonders what species this dead thing is.

Then a word rises unbidden to its lips.

'Human,' it whispers.

Fifty Mile Bone Beach

I am the Collector—she who sieves the shores of the Fifty Mile Bone Beach. A beach where the yellowed skeletons of long-dead whales lie scattered, pounded by ash-coloured waves and cradled in graves of plastic debris—the legacy of the last generation. An arc of crimson sky frames all.

Red.

Always red.

I hitch my satchel higher. Today's gathered trinkets clatter gently within. Some are useful for the community, others I choose for sentimental reasons.

The coil of frayed rope for instance, found tangled around a whale's jaw, will be given to the fisher crews; the cracked spinning top with its faded colours to the baby daughter of The Widow. Her husband disappeared in last week's fishing expedition.

Dangerous work in these dark waters.

But there is a rusted wrench I found also. Useless, but it reminds me of my father—a car mechanic before he died in the asteroid's deluge now fifty years gone. And a heart-shaped bone that recalls to me my mother and the beat of her heart against my ear. I have no photos of my family.

I cough. My old lungs are weak from half a century of inhaling the dust of ruined continents. At least here by the sea, beauty—although derelict—is still evident. I adjust my helmet and breather. The straps bite deep around my withered cheeks and press into the back of my skull. I suck in a breath, taking what pleasure I can from it. But there isn't much. The scrubbers filter the grit from the air, but not the scent of rotting seaweed and rubbish.

I step over a whale's rib bone, pitted and scored by its years on the beach. I slither across a patch of salt-slick stone. The next step, my boot disturbs a pile of debris—mud-laced sand and rainbow fragments of old plastic. A square edge of ebony emerges. Rectangular. Man-made.

My gloved fingers gently brush away the rubbish. It's a plastic bag with a flat plate within, imprinted with the symbol of a bitten apple. Apples. I salivate at the thought. They no longer exist, but I did eat them as a child. I relish the memory of their firm flesh, eaten fresh and cold on bright summer days.

I lift the bag clear of the sand—it's not a plate inside, I see now, but a bit of old-world tech.

A mobile phone.

I ease the bag open. Inside the phone rests scratched and scuffed. I take it out and turn it over, thumbing away a thin layer of sand as I do. I lift the edge to my eye. The connector is rusted. But no matter. The unit is in pretty good shape—maybe good enough to make an extraction.

I drop the plastic bag back to the beach and dig into my satchel. I pull free the chip bank I keep there for the rare occasions I find technology still intact. I also pull out a screwdriver and press the flat end into the seamed edge of the phone's case. It cracks open easily, like an eggshell.

The circuits inside are unbroken.

I smile and unclip the data board. The green of it is a colour I have not seen for a long time. Bright. Fresh. Alive.

The metal components are brown with corrosion, but it's still worth a try. I press the board into the chip bank with a firm *click*. The viewscreen flips up and a blue line of light indicates the uploading of data.

My heart thumps with anticipation. You never know what you are going to get with old tech. Sometimes it's a piece of music long forgotten, or the picture of a person who lived in a different time. Sometimes it's the fragment of a book—called an e-book in those days.

Sometimes you get nothing at all.

The chip bank beeps. The viewscreen flickers and then, pixel by pixel, an image of the data within the phone's board starts to form.

There isn't much. There never is.

But this time I am gifted a photograph.

A single photograph.

An old-world photograph.

My eyes widen as the content builds. The image is painted in brilliant shades of blue, yellow and white—it's a beach. The surf, sand, waves and sky are the sort of which have long gone from Earth. I glimpse the snow-white breast of a gull hovering on a sea breeze so crisp I can almost taste it. Foam from crashing waves clings to clean sand and sunlight sparks diamonds off a sapphire sea. In the far distance tower buildings larger than any that exist now. Glittering, mirrored monoliths that reach up to clutch the sky.

Tears prick the back of my eyes. I press my tongue to the roof of my mouth. I was only a small child when it was all taken away. I had forgotten how beautiful it was—forgotten all that was lost.

I turn to glance back at my current home—the small village that clings to the grim cliffs and battered beach.

And it is such a far cry from those soaring buildings of old, and the beach is not the bright expanse our ancestors enjoyed. It is bitter and barely hospitable, with the houses built from a patchwork of old tech married to whale bones and debris.

Our existence is small.

It is humble.

I look back at the photograph. Part of me wishes I hadn't been reminded of how it once was.

With the screwdriver, I pry the board from the chip bank. The image blinks away. I slot it and the reader into my satchel for safekeeping. My gaze swings across the bone beach and on to the dark sea stretching beyond.

I smile.

I at least have my ocean.

My ocean of derelict beauty.

SHORT ARC TRANSFERENCE

It's shaped like a bullet, but looks like a tomb. The sleek ship, *Ghosthunter*, its distress beacon flashing every three seconds, floats listlessly in orbit around the dead, orange planet designated as XX32-5. As the hull turns into the light thrown by the planet's single sun, lines of strange black symbols are revealed, etched into the metal. The marks look as if they are slithering, moving to keep in the light. But I say nothing. My reality is compromised. It's safer to distrust anything that appears strange.

'I don't like the look of this, Tesha,' says Kyllan, 'and you know I've got a good nose for trouble.'

I glance at my brother and press my lips together. 'For getting into it.'

He grins, teeth white against his creased, ruddy skin.

'Besides,' I say, 'we're getting paid a lot to find this ship and bring her people home.'

'Money ain't everything.'

I shrug. It is for me. I still own the fleshy brain I was born with. Stupid, considering the available tech, but I've never had the credits to get an upgrade. Now, at sixty years old, it's failing me. Early-stage dementia.

It's modernise or die.

But Kyllan doesn't need to know that. Not while there's a chance to make it go away. So I appeal to the wanton side of his nature.

'Money matters if you wanna eat,' I say.

Kyllan pats his rounded belly. 'I do like to eat.'

'Well, it's time for a spacewalk then. Wouldn't want you starving.'

'I'll get your suit ready.' Kyllan wiggles his greying eyebrows, flashes another grin and heads down to the cargo bay airlock.

I glance back at the stricken vessel. The case notes say it's used to run tours for rich folk out to ancient, ruined cities on alien worlds.

Why would anyone do that?

It's dangerous out here on the fringes of space.

Too easy to lose yourself.

***

I reach *Ghosthunter* without incident. My grav boots lock me onto the metal hull with a dull clang. The airlock hatch door is free from the curling black symbols that cover the rest of the ship. I spin the hatch mechanism and it opens easily. Blue-white sensor lights illuminate as I glide across the threshold. I twist, floating in the airless space, and tap the activator panel by the door. The hatch closes with a soft sigh and the vents hiss, filling the room with oxygen. Gravity activates and my boots hit the floor with a thud. I tap my comms bracelet.

'I'm in, Kyllan.'

'Suit systems are all green-lined, Sis. You are good to go.' Kyllan's voice sounds tinny through the communication bud in my ear.

The inside hatch opens out to reveal an interior corridor. Twelve doors line the wall on the opposite side. The head-up display in my visor lists atmospheric conditions.

'How's it looking?' asks Kyllan.

'Atmosphere's breathable, and we got gravity.'

I unclip my suit gloves. My helmet releases next with a click. The air in the ship smells stale.

'CO_2 scrubbers are offline though,' I say. 'See if you can connect to the on-board systems and restart them.'

'Aye,' comes the reply.

I tuck the gloves into the helmet and ease down the corridor. This looks like the accommodations deck of the ship. The doors, all open, lead to lush apartments fitted out in tones of grey, white and blue—a clean, sleek aesthetic. Each room is neat but unoccupied. Inside, blue emergency lights pulse on and off, a repeating pattern. The EVAC warning system has been set off. Maybe the passengers got out.

A ship access panel is set into the wall at the end of the corridor. I tap up the escape pod inventory. All are still accounted for.

Where the hell are they?

A gut feeling tells me it isn't anywhere good. I bite my lip and brush my fingertips across the blaster holstered at my side. The weapon lends me a measure of comfort. I call up the ship's deck plans. Two levels to this vessel with a small cargo bay at the rear. Control bridge is above me. I'll start there. The plush carpet floors mask the sound of my steps as I head for the elevator. I trail my fingers along the wall as I walk. The metal feels warm.

Strange.

***

I find the bodies on the bridge. Ten of them. Nine men and one woman. The bloated corpses lie on their backs in a circle, heads all facing towards the centre. Each one has a spent blue candle melted to the floor by their feet. The thick wax cylinders look ancient and are marked with an overlapped cross-and-circle-shaped symbol. Over the bodies the ship's viewscreen is active, showing the orange planet outside glaring down like a sickly eye.

And the inner hull. It's covered in the same black symbols found on the exterior of the ship. The marks writhe as if trying to break free of the surface. I press my palms to my temples. Hallucinations again. They aren't new to me, being a common symptom of my affliction. What I wouldn't give for a machine-made brain now. For a moment longer, I battle the image of seething, tattooed metal walls.

You are just imagining it…

Holy fuck but it looks real…

Finally, it eases. The walls resolve and I lower shaking hands. My sense of self-preservation screams at me to run but I force logic to win out—running won't earn me the credits I need.

The CO_2 scrubbers engage. A rush of fresh air enters the room from the ceiling vents and begins to circulate. With it comes a sweep of pungent odour. I hold my glove to my nose. It's kicked up from the bodies. Not surprising. By the greenish hue to their flesh, these people have been lying here for a few days at least. Morbid curiosity pulls me closer.

The same cross and circle symbol on the candles is scorched into the forehead of each corpse. No blood, just a cauterised wound like a laser-blade would make. Another body, a man dressed in a chrome-bright suit, sits apart from the circle. He leans back, half slumped in the captain's chair. His corpse seems fresher than the rest, as if he's only just died. The hole in his temple, showing the shredded wires of his upgraded mechanical brain, and the blaster in his hand suggests he killed himself. I lean in closer. He is marked like the others but his eyes look different— moist-looking black orbs without irises, open and staring at the planet in the viewscreen.

On his lap rests another candle and a flat square of dull silver metal. The same strange symbols on the hull are repeated on the surface of the plate. The cross and circle features amongst them. I consider the marks. An alien language maybe? I take a photo with my helmet cam and transfer it to Kyllan.

'Unknown dialect,' comes back his reply.

The orange planet glowers at me from the viewscreen. A sudden thought strikes. Could the plate and candles be relics from the ruins down there?

I tap my comms. 'Kyllan.'

'Let me guess. All dead?'

'Yup.' I engage my helmet view cam and send the feed back to the ship.

'Holy hell,' says Kyllan. 'What happened to them, do ya think?'

'Not sure.' I point the camera to the plate. 'I'm thinking the planet might have some answers.'

'Risky to go down there.'

He isn't wrong. 'The families will want to know what happened. I'll see if *Ghosthunter's* ship-to-surface vessel is intact and head down.'

'Come back here and we'll go together.'

'Nah. I need you up here in case something goes wrong.'

He isn't happy about it, obvious by the heavy sigh he breathes into the mic. But he knows better than to disagree with me.

'Right'o, Tesha. But be careful.'

'Aye.'

I take the plate and candle from the dead man's lap. They might come in handy down on the planet. As I do, the corpse shudders. I step back, heart beating unsteady against my ribs. The carved marking on the man's forehead glows green and he blinks slowly, once. His head turns stiffly. Black eyes, now laced with green fire, find mine.

'I've been waiting,' he says, words slurred around a bloated tongue.

I step back. The items, still in my hand, feel heavy.

'This body fought me. Its mind was—unnatural,' whispers the dead man.

The metal plate shivers. I gasp as the symbols on the surface start to move. They run off the edge of the metal and seep into my skin. I freeze as the alien letters, letters that whisper of souls and transfers, burrow into my flesh. Their touch is both ice and adrenaline.

Alien thoughts fill my mind.

Yes. A host much better suited to my needs.

***

I run down the passageway. The black symbols in the walls follow as I go, sliding across the metal skin like ink over water. My mind has not felt so clear in years. I need to get to the planet. The metal plate and candle are tucked neatly into the largest of my suit's pockets. Their weight bounces against my leg as I make my way to the cargo bay and the ship-to-surface vessel that should be there. I pull at the neck of my suit. When did it get so hot in here?

The black symbols pause, pulsing, on the cargo bay entry door. Yes. This is the right way. I hasten, grav boots clanging against the grated deck. The activator panel beeps on my approach and the door slides open, revealing a dark hanger. I grasp the doorframe, and a finger brushes one of the bird-shaped black symbols. Behind me, a woman cries out. I swing around to find nothing but shadows and tattooed metal.

'Who's there?'

The alien thoughts fill my mind again.

The relics must be returned to the temple. The invaders deserved what they got—souls trapped. The Repository of Knowledge is not theirs. The wisdom of elders is held in the metal, how can we flourish without it?

I close my eyes and focus on resetting an internal equilibrium. These thoughts are not my own. More hallucinations. I suck in an urgent breath. In my mind an overlay of images presents—the orange planet, desolate and dry but then green and rich with life. I shake my head. I've only ever seen it dead.

No. Green. Alive. It can be so again.

I push the foreign thought away and slip into the cargo bay. Behind me the woman cries out again. I ignore it. I'll get the metal plate back to the planet and then get the hell out of this damned galaxy and back to an organ-upgrade facility. This brain of mine is more fucked up than I thought.

The motion sensor lights in the cargo bay turn on as I enter. The symbols slide past the door's frame and settle to cover the hanger's walls. The sleek little ship-to-surface vessel sits docked slightly askew at the centre of the room. The gangplank waits, ready. I race across the deck.

Yes, yes, murmur the thoughts in my head. *Take us home.*

'It's not your home,' says another voice—a real voice.

I pause on the gangplank and turn. It's the woman I saw dead on the bridge. She is there—and is not. Her translucent figure hovers just off the hull, a ghost straining to be clear of the wall. But as she fights, her skirts keep her tied back to the metal by thin strings of the black symbols. They stretch out taut behind her, shapes deformed but resolute in their strength to bind her.

The woman speaks again, the mark on her forehead illuminated by the same green light that lit the dead man's eyes in the captain's chair.

'She failed here,' says the woman. 'The spirit in the metal plate. The alien. We took her from the ruins on the planet below and she tried to use us to rebuild her race.' Her face turns away. 'We fought her.'

I blink. Another hallucination?

Yes.

The shadow woman wrings her hands. 'Please don't go. She's bound us to the metal. Release our souls.'

The symbols on the walls shudder. They stretch and mutate as other shadowy figures strain clear from the walls. Ten and then one more—

Ghosthunter's lost passengers and crew.

My bile rises. I swallow it back.

Let us leave. Alien thoughts again. *You are sick. Come. I will heal you and then you will heal my world.*

A vision fills my mind of a great, orange desert plain guarded by tall grey-skinned beings. Sleeping humans lay arranged into circles. Blue candles, each set on a metal plate etched with black symbols, burn at their feet. Each flame flickers hungrily, drawing ephemeral light away from the bodies—soul-light siphoned off and transferred through wax to metal. The alien beings move through the bodies with laser-blades, reaching down to carve a mark in each forehead—a cross and circle. A darker light seeps down from each mark to inhabit the empty corpse.

And then the bodies rise. Their eyes solid black and backlit with green light.

See? whispers the voice in my head. *Your kind sacrificed to save mine.*

I clench my teeth and rip my blaster free from the holster.

'Fuck that,' I mutter.

***

The spirit in my mind clamps down and I buckle under the weight of her presence. On my knees, I'm forced to reach for the metal plate and candle in my pocket. My fingers fumble on the clasps that hold it closed. But it gives and the relics clatter to the floor. I sob. Again my will is overridden. The candle is lifted and placed on the metal. It flickers alight.

I clench my fists and wrestle with the presence in my head. For a moment I win clear of her. I press my blaster to the plate. My brain burns as the alien realises what I am doing. She rages. I squeeze the trigger.

Blast.

Blast.

Blast.

The candle rolls away as my ammunition clip clicks over empty. The plate hasn't even buckled. The ghost woman from the wall has disappeared but her voice still resonates from within the hull.

'Don't give up!'

Desperate, I slam my blaster against the plate. The alien presence screeches in my brain. The butt of the weapon rebounds and slips. My palm falls and connects with the metal. At the touch, black symbols re-form on my skin. They slide away from me and back onto the metal plate. The alien laughs and the clear-headedness I'd felt fades.

Why am I here? Who am I?

Somewhere in the back of my mind, I imagine a familiar voice screams at me to get back to the airlock. I know that voice. Kyllan?

But a woman is calling me too. She sounds desperate.

I want to help her. She's trapped in the hull.

I get to my feet and stumble past a blue candle and to the wall. Maybe if I dig at it, I can scratch her out. My nails bite into the metal but it somehow feels too soft. I slip and fall through it.

A woman catches me. Her tears are warm on my cheek.

'I'm sorry,' she whimpers. 'I should have let you go.'

The woman looks past me. I turn to follow her gaze. A barrier made of black curling symbols ripples between the outside world and me. I press against it and it gives slightly. Outside, an old woman stands facing me. She wears my face; well, almost. Her eyes are solid black—alien eyes—eyes backlit with a strange green light.

She presses a finger to her comms bracelet.

'Everything is fine here, Kyllan. How about you come on over and we'll go down to the planet together.'

'Just a hallucination,' I whisper.

A Pitcher of Water at the End of Days

'Aquarius?'

The name my mother gave me—in the hope that I would adopt the traits of the sun sign—concludes too much. I am no airy-minded dreamer. I am a space explorer. And one focused on fighting to survive.

'Aquarius?' My husband, Aeon, calls out again. His voice cracks, throat thick with the red dust that gathers in the air. I glance up from the blanket panels I am joining and out the shuttle's port window. My fingers still work the metal needles as I watch the blood-dark dust storm crouching on the horizon.

'In the control room,' I reply.

Aeon's boots thud up the metal ladder. Muscled and barrel-chested, he squeezes into the cockpit. He is too large for the small space and his body knows it. I can tell in the way he holds his shoulders hunched forward.

He looks weary, only half the man he was when he flew us out from Space Dock 10. His cheeks are heavy with lines and his bright blue eyes are dulled to grey. Even his uniform looks tired, holes and oil stains marring the knees. 'You got that blanket ready?'

I knot the last thread and snip it with the pliers from the console. 'Yeah. Ready.'

'Good.' He dips his head to look out the window and rubs his dusty knuckles under his nose. I notice blood on his wrist, the place where perhaps a wrench tore a hole as he fixed the sub-thrusters. Watching the approaching dust storm, he nods. 'It'll be here soon. Better go cover the condensers.'

I lay my weaving needles aside and fold the blanket into quarters. 'On it,' I say.

***

The air outside smells like petroleum, bitter and burning on the back of my tongue. I swallow, trying to remove the taste, but it sticks there. I clutch the blanket to my chest as I head along the side of the craft. Its giant silver hull towers over me like a metal cliff. Scrapes mar the bright steel, scars earned in our forced landing three days ago. Most of the damage is to the rear of the ship. As I approach it, I see Aeon has been busy. The sub-thruster plates are back in place, meaning the focusing crystal cradles have already been re-aligned.

I move past the plates and on to the condensers. Work is ongoing here. The medium sized units, with their shallow funnels and wide turbines, are exposed from behind broken hatches. Usually used to convert ice molecules from interstellar dust into fuel, the components now collect and process water from sand particles. Both units are covered in a thick layer of dust. Too much dust. Not ideal for the working mechanisms and as our only source of water, all the more reason to get them covered before the storm hits.

The breeze kicks up as I approach the units. The storm moves closer. Shards of lightning skitter and circle the dense mass of dark air hanging low in the distance. I turn my face away from the stinging grains of sand carried on the wind. Grit crunches between my teeth. There is a bad feeling to this storm. Uneasy, I unfold the ion blanket I pieced together from four separate sheets. The interwoven metal links clink as I tuck the edges into place around the condensers. I reach into my vest and grab my pocket welder. A green light flicks on when I activate it. The glowing tip makes short work of fusing the blanket to the hull.

I look up and notice the quality of the light has changed. The bright daylight from the planet's three suns has dimmed to dark orange. With the suns obscured behind the approaching dust cloud, the landscape is suddenly far more ominous.

Aeon waits at the gangplank. His broad hand reaches down for me. The wind grows wilder, snapping at my hair. 'Hurry up!' he says, 'We need to secure the hatch.'

I start to run.

I almost reach his hand.

But the dust beats me.

With a sudden drop in atmospheric pressure, the storm is on us. I am flung from the gangway and tossed against the ship's landing strut. Pain lances along my ribcage but soon fades. I look for Aeon. He is still on the gangplank. In shock, I watch him turn and stumble back into the cargo bay. The shuttle door grinds shut. *Is he leaving me out here to die?* All I can do is clutch at my anchor.

I never thought Aeon to be a coward.

My thoughts circle. Perhaps he only left Earth for the glory, to find evidence of alien species to further his own career. Maybe it was never about us taming the universe together. Maybe I was just a contingency plan—something to sacrifice if it was needed.

My anger sits like a rock in my belly.

And the wind is just as angry. It roars around me, twisting and turning like the currents of Earth's far oceans. Waves of sand buffet against me. I squeeze my eyes shut against the stinging onslaught, but the backs of my hands, cheeks and neck suffer the brunt of its vicious touch.

I sob.

Damn Aeon. Damn him to hell. I'm going to die out here.

I force my eyes open to a blurred view of lightning lashing against the dark sky. It is almost beautiful, the way the edges of the electricity skitter and are shattered by the errant winds. Squinting, I look to the ship. Panels are peeling off the hull like scales torn from a fish. I watch them twist up into the sky, before they are thrown away like ruined toys.

A shriek of metal. I glance back at the gangway. The door to the ship opens and Aeon, dressed in his space suit, emerges. My heart leaps. He hasn't abandoned me.

His steps are laboured as his huge bulk presses against the force of the storm. I sob again, feeling guilty for doubting him. He is carrying something. Metal winks in his gloved hand. Another ion blanket.

My desperation turns to hope. If he can get the blanket to me, I can make it to the ship. I close my eyes, huddle my chin to my chest and with hair whipping around my head like serpents, I wait for Aeon.

His hand is like a vice on my shoulder. I look up and see myself reflected in the mirrored surface of his helmet's visor. The blanket falls over my shoulders and head and the stinging of the sand fades. Aeon pulls me to my feet and leads me towards the gangway. The wind pounds our backs, pushing us up towards the open door. I reach out and grasp the pillar. I turn to Aeon. But as I do, he slips. I can't see his face, but I sense his desperation in the way he grips at my arm. But his gloves give him little purchase. His fingers slip, his boots scrape on the gangway and then he is torn away for me.

I watch in horror as he is pulled upward into the sky. Gusts of wind, spinning like a tornado, fling him against the back of the storm like a broken doll.

Then he is gone.

I make it back into the ship. I press the button and the door closes. The forces of nature fade to a distant sound rattling against the hull. I sit with my back against the door and cry.

***

The ship will never fly again, but the condensers survived the storm. Heart-sore and weary, I pull away the blankets that held the units safe. Aeon's laser cutter, pilfered from his toolbox, fires up at a touch of the button. He always looked after what belonged to him. Guilt washes over me again at the thought.

The cutter sears the condensers free from their cradles. They thump to the ground, moisture leaking out from their collection canisters. I sit the unit up and trickle a handful of sand into the funnel. The turbines grind as they spin, but still water begins to form on the blades. I breathe a sigh of relief. They still work.

I get to my feet and lift the unit to my shoulder. It's heavy, but its value on a world like this is priceless. I look up into the now clear sky. The three suns blaze down on my forehead. I close my eyes then open them again. Time to go. I step away from the ship and head towards the distant horizon. If I am lucky, I will find the aliens we came looking for. Perhaps they might find my gift of water a fair trade for my life. Or perhaps this may be the End of Days for me.

As I walk, heading for the far horizon, I am struck by the irony that on this desert planet, I have become what my mother named me for. A woman holding a pitcher of water on her shoulder. I have become Aquarius, the Water Bearer.

RUSTED WINGS

The rusted dragon lies in the back alley, half-buried in a pile of mouldy crates. I ease my way along the salt-damp walls of the inn, clinging to the shadows. The whale-oil lamps throw puddles of dirty yellow light at intervals across the scene, a canvas of mustard yellows, blacks and sodden grey. My bag clinks quietly at my side. It's dangerous to be here—to want to try and save this machine. But I feel a connection to him. He is alone and abandoned, an orphan just like me. But I need to be careful. He is contrary, and for good reason. Many have tried to loot his parts in the past, but even downed, he defends himself admirably.

The pile of bones stacked next to him attest to that.

I creep forward. My boot scuffs the ground.

'I can smell you, human,' creaks an eroded voice. 'Reveal yourself.' The dragon's tarnished head lifts off the black flagstones. His eyes burn like embers in his discoloured face and his metal lips peel back to reveal rows of half-broken copper teeth.

I step out from the shadows. 'I'm not here to loot you,' I say. 'I'm here to help.'

The dragon's eyes narrow. 'Help? I've seen you before. You're a common thief, girl. You can't help me.' He turns away as if the conversation is done.

'I know your name is Quisyn,' I say.

The dragon shrugs. 'So?'

'You fought in the Diamond Wars.'

'Been speaking to the whaler crews have you? Aye, they have much courage in their cups. Telling my tale over their tankards, as if they earned it themselves.'

'They said you were the old king's personal steed.'

Quisyn shuffles. His claws screech. The jagged edges of his broken wing pistons scrape along the ground.

'It suited me to let him ride, for it takes a king to keep me flying. Are you a king, little girl?'

I venture another step closer. 'No. Not a king. But someone with an understanding of machines.' I point to my shoulder bag, the last gift my father, Holt, a master oilsmith, gave me before he died. 'And I have tools. If you will allow it, I would like to try and fix you so you can fly again. You deserve better than rotting here.'

'What do you know of the things I deserve?'

'I heard you fought for the humans when the rest of your kind deserted us. We owe you as I figure it.'

'And yet the betrayal of humans has seen me grounded here. Your kind killed the king and with the spilling of his blood, took my wings from me.'

'Not all of us are bad. Please let me try.'

The dragon lifts his head. Two trails of ebony smoke rise from his nostrils, bleak shadows staining the air. 'Come and look then…if you dare.'

The air hangs thick by him, heavy with the stench of rotting bones and decaying steel. I kneel, breathing shallow as I inspect him. Rusted bolts line his sides and his scales, said to be once bright, are brown with edges frayed. I unsling my bag and rest it on the ground. The precious metal tools within rattle gently. I turn to examine the dragon's face. The lamp above him catches the broken lens in his left eye. I shudder.

'Do you fear me?' asks Quisyn.

'No.'

'Then you are braver than most.'

I shrug. 'My pa used to say it wasn't bravery, but stupidity from a heart born too big.'

'My king always said that big hearts save lives,' whispers Quisyn, almost to himself.

Quisyn's hide is a mess of corrosion. Flakes of rust fall away as I lift his wing to the side. Metal shrieks—his ailerons sliding against each other. My heart sinks. His decay is too far beyond my skill to fix.

The dragon's gaze has not left me. His eyes, so ancient, read my thoughts skilfully. 'Do not be disappointed. You are not the first to come and fail,' he says. 'Blacksmiths, diesel workers, magicians have all preceded you. Each had grand plans of how they would use me to better their lots in life. But truth is, without a king, I'll never fly again.'

'Why must it be a king?' I ask. 'Why can't anyone else do it?'

The dragon smiles, his ragged, ruined grin terrifying. 'Why do you want to know?'

'Because I want to help you get away from here. This alley is no place to die.'

The dragon tilts his head. 'You are not here for personal gain?'

'I'm a thief. I take what I need. I don't rely on anybody else.'

'What makes you think I want to rely on you?'

I shrug. 'Because you've got nothin' to lose.'

Quisyn seems satisfied with my answer. He swings his snout towards me and opens his mouth, exposing a black maw and the dimly glowing cylinder of his throat. His mouth closes again. 'See? I need a king because only embers remain in my heart forge. My fire is almost out.'

'I can start a new fire for you. You don't need no high-and-mighty lord for that.'

'But it is no ordinary fire I need.'

'Then what?'

The dragon's eyes flare then fade. He frowns, the hinged scales around his mouth scraping quietly as they shift. 'My kind need diamonds. Only their icy facets can feed our charmed fire, and in this country only kings possess such gems.'

Diamonds?

If diamonds are the answer, then Quisyn is right. He'll never fly. The old king's diamond mines were destroyed by fire in the same battle that killed him.

A sound rattles at the far end of the alleyway. A silhouette slips past the piles of rubbish, bared briefly against the glow of the oil lamps. Quisyn's nose ripples. A low growl rumbles in his throat. 'You had better leave now, young one.' His eyes narrow. 'There is a stench in the air that does not bode well. Go hide. And take my thanks with you. Not many come these days that care.'

I nod and pick up my bag. 'I'll return soon.'

The dragon's gaze slews sideways to lock on mine. 'Only if you bear diamonds,' he says, the ghost of a smile touching his lips. 'Now, go!'

My boots skid as I scuttle away. Footsteps echo out louder behind me. A chill creeps down my spine and I realise I can't clear the far end of the alley in time. I duck behind a pile of firewood sacks, crouch down and peer around the corner.

Quisyn shifts, pushing his broken wings into the road to lift him higher. His neck arches and a bellow of smoke, blacker than before, blossoms out of his nostrils. He falls back, exhausted.

'My, my Quisyn,' says a voice as cold as ice. 'How far you have fallen.'

A figure steps out of the darkness. A black cloak conceals the face, but the hands, milk-white and soft are visible resting on the pommel of a fine, silver sword. Next to it hangs a smaller blade, a dagger with a golden handle.

The blades would be worth a year's coin if I could find a way to swipe them.

The dragon's chin lifts, the elegance of the movement contradicting the ruined tragedy of his body. 'I am fallen,' he says, 'But I remain loyal to my king.'

'Your king died a long time ago.'

'But not the principles he lived for. Peace reigns even in his absence.'

'Under the rule of a false king! When my brother died, the throne should have been mine. Join me and I will resurrect you. Help me reclaim my rightful place.'

'No,' says Quisyn. 'Your path is lined with blood. You are not fit to rule. My answer remains the same as it has every year you come—I will not pledge loyalty to you.'

'You betray my family.'

Quisyn takes a deep breath. Sorrow settles heavy in the forged lines of his face. 'Never,' he says. 'I am here, a broken relic of a broken past. You are here, a broken woman with a broken mind. The last wishes of your brother will be honoured—I will not fight a foreign king that rules peacefully in your stead. Your twisted mind would destroy this kingdom given reign.'

The hooded figure throws back its cloak. A woman, thin and lithe, emerges dressed in vivid green breeches and doublet—expensive textiles coloured with arsenic by the fabric weavers. The cascade of fire-red hair curling down her back marks her as a member of the fallen royal family, the Essans.

I gasp. She is the dead king's sister. Her face graced a painting I once stole from a merchant. She is the Mad Princess, Marlaina Essan.

Marlaina leans in to the dragon. Her hair tumbles over one shoulder; the lamplight catches the brilliant white of her teeth as she bares them.

'You are a traitor.' She draws the dagger from her belt, the fine steel ringing as it pulls clear. The slim blade glitters brightly against the grittiness of the alley—a work of art framed by debris and waste.

The dragon's eyes widen with a longing barely contained. I lean out further to see why. Then I realise—it's not the blade shining, but the hundreds of diamonds that line its length.

'You would recognise my brother's own dagger,' sneers Marlaina. 'Look upon it and weep. This blade would sustain you for a thousand years.'

Quisyn looks away. 'I would rather rot.'

Marlaina plunges the dagger back into her belt. 'This is your last chance, dragon. I will not return here again.'

'Go, Mad Princess,' says Quisyn, his voice edged like broken glass. 'I shall not lament the loss of your company.'

'Suit yourself!' Marlaina snarls. She wheels away. Her footsteps grow louder as she approaches my hiding spot. I roll back into the friendly shadows listening to her frustrated mutterings as she stalks past.

A flash of green.

A rolling swath of black fabric as her cloak follows.

The glint of a diamond dagger.

I can't help myself. I am a thief, and a damned fine one at that.

I reach out, my heart in my mouth but fingers steady.

A flick.

The dagger slips from the belt to rest cool in my hand.

The Mad Princess, oblivious, keeps walking until the shadows consume her.

I smile.

***

Quisyn's head rests defeated on the flagstones. His conversation with the princess seems to have stolen his fire. But even so, his tone with me is firm. 'I told you to leave.'

'I did. And then I came back.'

'Why?'

'Because I haven't given up on you.'

The dragon lifts his head. 'Leave me to decay in peace, child.' He sighs. 'There is no helping. The sooner I'm done, the happier I shall be.'

'But what if I *could* help? What would you do if you had your freedom?'

Quisyn's side bellows out as he draws in breath. 'I would leave this place,' he says. 'Return to the mountain kingdom where my kind dwells. There I would feed to full on diamonds and live free.'

Freedom. A place away from the filth of the city. A dream after my own heart.

'Would you take me?'

Quisyn chuckles, a sad sound divulging the truth of dreams long abandoned. 'If we could go, what would you trade with me for passage? My kind does nothing for free.'

I draw the stolen dagger out from under my jerkin. Its diamonds fracture the lamplight, casting dapples of rainbow light across my hand. 'This.'

Quisyn's eyes widen, round like luminous moons. 'What...? How...?'

'You said to come back with diamonds.'

A growl reverberates deep in the dragon's body. It rises and rises, a terrifying, thunderous sound that sets the crates around him to rocking. The dragon is laughing.

'My clever little thief,' says Quisyn. 'For that blade, I will take you anywhere you wish.'

I smile. 'Then it's yours, if I can come with you.'

Quisyn takes the dagger gently into his mouth. His broken teeth crunch down. The diamonds shatter.

And colour blossoms across his metal. Rust falls away to reveal new steel, silver and clean and bright—scales with razor edges. His wings extend, the parts reforming and rebuilding like magic before my eyes. Rubbish falls away from his hide in a curtain. His eyes blaze and his mouth opens, his throat a glaring luminous blue.

'Climb aboard,' he says, his voice now lyrical and sharp edged.

And I do. The dragon pushes off, his wingtips scraping at the alley walls. Then we are airborne.

We are free.

An orphaned thief and a metal dragon—

A dragon with diamond dust falling from his teeth.

TERRALIGHT

F ive Driller teams dead so far. Mining for grey fuel on Amarion-5 has ground to a halt. Why do the Hegemon authorities always wait so long to call me in?

I tap the communicator button at my wrist. The red signal light shows an active connection.

'Amarion-5 Off World Base,' I say. 'Cyanna Ryan confirming landing. Ship damaged. Require transport assistance for return. Please acknowledge.' I wait. Static hisses from the speakers in reply.

I try again. 'Please acknowledge.' More static. I sigh. Some kind of magnetic interference. I'll need to find higher ground to improve the connection.

I look out across the sea of shifting, orange sands. The planet doesn't look like much, but you can never tell which ones will choose to fight back. Usually it's the younger ones that prove to be a problem for the Hegemon—they still hold a greater awareness of themselves. But Amarion-5 is old, she is still awake, and she is defiant.

She has created a spectre army to see to her defence. The reason I have been called in. I can't say I blame her. This planet's peoples were murdered; slaughtered so her rivers of grey fuel could be mined to power Hegemon starships.

If I were such a planet, hell, I'd fight back too. I feel sorry for Amarion-5, but I'll end the planet's rebellion to further Hegemon interests. It's what they pay me to do, after all.

Sometimes I wonder if that makes me a priestess or a murderer. The gods know I've been called both in my time.

I look back towards the wreckage of my shuttle. The small ship lies half-buried in the desert sand. I was lucky to make it down intact. A low-orbit collision with satellite debris has left the shuttle hull scarred and battered. I turn away. The vessel did its job by making the landing but now it's useless. Just another skeleton that will be left to rot in the heat of the desert sun.

I squint at the horizon. The same breeze that ruffles my hair blows across the ocean of sand. And not only the sand. The fluid plains are dotted with stone ruins and stunted purple thorn bushes, shedding their pollen as grey dust into the thin air. It is a grim, bleak landscape telling a story of wreckage. The cloudless sky that arcs overhead is an ominous wash of dark mustard, the colour of a half-healed bruise.

For a moment I wonder what this place looked like before the Hegemon mining crews invaded, before it was changed from a *Level 1: Habitable* planet to a *Level 9: Dead-Zone*. But I do not let my imagination reign. Years of experience have taught me that to consider what *was*, against the canvas of what *is*, is the surest way to heartbreak.

I unclip the hand-held onnocular from my belt. Through it, the planet's view is magnified. More thorns, lonely broken buildings and sand. I click down the scanner lens. Green laser lines crisscross the viewscreen. A list of numbers cycles down the right side. Atmospheric composition, ground temperature, air toxicity and humidity. The results concur with my ship's scans. Air breathable, no water. Fine by me. I'll only be here a short while.

I drop my gaze to the last number on the list—the spectre-plasm readings. They spike in concentration to the north. I increase the onnocular's magnification. A blunt-edged stone ridge sharpens into view.

The height I need for my comms to work will be there. And beyond it will be why I've come.

I clip the onnocular back onto my belt and re-adjust the terrablade resting in the holster at my side. The distant ridge is a smear on the horizon. It's a fair way out but, armed and with my water canister full, I can make it.

As I walk, the planet's distress becomes obvious. Its acid emotions leech from the ground, rising—poisonous—through the soles of my boots. The bone deep ache infects my knees, elbows and teeth. I clench my fists. All planets over-soaked in blood emanate like this. It doesn't bode well for what I'll find over the ridge.

And what that is, I have seen a hundred times before on a hundred different worlds. Armies of the dead, riled with self-righteous purpose and having already lost their lives, fighting with nothing else to lose. A spirit will lead them, one who in life was respected. Sometimes a warrior, other times an elder. That is the phantom to watch, the one who leads the pack. The receptacle of the planet's purpose in working to ensure victory at all cost.

But even so empowered, those shades are not indestructible.

In all my years, I have never yet suffered a defeat.

I grasp the hilt of my terrablade. The weapon is the secret to my successes, a weapon that can both disperse spirits and subdue the core of an unquiet planet. Its solid weight bounces against my side as I walk, reminding me of my purpose. *Secure the planet at all cost.* But with purpose comes danger, and wielding the weapon's tech is hazardous. Modified hydrogen atoms impregnated into the metal, when activated to become terralight, can draw off a wielder's own spirit—if that wielder is not careful.

Experience has made me cautious. I am careful to avoid its use merely to settle the smaller, less important tragedies I pass—the shade of the twin-horned, horse-like creature wandering the dunes, driven by the memory of a terrible thirst; or the Hegemon soldier who sits against a broken wall with his legs missing, his shade calling pitifully for his mother.

Without the danger, the priestess in me would ease their lingering, but the murderer is more practical. I see no use in risking my life to solve problems that are not my own.

***

The orange and yellow ridge is relatively easy to climb. Horizontal leaves of stone, stacked like books and worn smooth by the wind-driven sand, act as steps. I look down as I walk, imagining what the final battle here would have sounded like—the cries, the moans of the dying. Had no-one heard the broken sobbing of a heart-sore world, unable to absorb any more blood, crying for it all to stop?

The wind rises as I crest the ridge. I squint against the sand that runs with it, hand up to protect my face. I step down from the small plateau and follow the faint track into the shallow valley below.

From here, I see this world was not always a desert. The remains of a river crawls towards the east. A silver-white forest of dead trees lines the cracked clay pan. Long, wicked spines sprout from pale branches, standing stiff against the elements. Their tips are hung with macabre wind chimes made from the armoured skeletons of Hegemon dead.

The bones dance and I sense eyes upon me. I scan my surrounds. The dirty, yellow light from the sky casts shadows against the white trees. Another gust of wind, the bones clatter again. Then the eyes reveal themselves. They belong to a woman who steps out of the forest across the river, an active terrablade held upright in her fierce grip.

I pull my own sword free of its scabbard. The hydrogen atoms in the weapon begin to glow red as they process the heightened levels of spectre-plasm in the air. The woman, dressed in the same severe dark grey uniform as myself, pauses at the centre of the dead river basin. Another elite Grey Guard Spirit Hunter.

'Do you live or do you linger?' she asks.

'I live,' I reply. 'You?'

The woman lifts her chin. Her eyes, a pale green, cut through me. Her glare is cold and calculating. I respect the scrutiny. Caution is the prerogative of any good hunter.

I seem to pass her test.

'I live,' she says, lowering her blade. Its glowing tip hovers just shy of the ground. 'Why are you here? The Hegemon contract for this world is mine.'

'You are mistaken,' I say. 'Amarion-5 was allocated to me.'

The woman's eyes thin. 'When?'

'Yesterday. I deployed this morning.'

The woman's eyebrows rise. 'You must be Cyanna Ryan then?'

'Correct.'

'Well, they'll be happy upstairs to hear you've arrived. I'm the Amarion-7 base station Hunter. When they didn't receive your landing confirmation this morning, they sent for me to find you and finish the job if need be.'

Amarion-7—the smaller sister planet to Amarion-5. It's close, but not that close. She must have been deployed from her own base as soon as I missed the landing confirmation. I'm surprised they sent someone so quickly, but then again the Hegemon is desperate for mining to begin again.

My fingers touch my communicator. 'Some issues with interference. I couldn't get through.'

The woman shrugs. 'Not to worry. Glad to have found you. It's probably a good thing to have two blades here anyway.' She points to the forest. 'With the amount of spectre-plasm here, we might be looking at a caging event.'

Caging. I frown. It's an unnatural use of the terralight power—a cruel, unholy way to end spirits already aggrieved by violent deaths. Never a first-action solution.

'Surely it won't come to that,' I say.

She walks up out of the riverbed and stops in front of me. 'I guess we can hope.'

'We more than hope. We work to avoid it.'

The woman's eyes narrow even as her lips crease into a cold smile. Unease crawls along my spine. Something about this woman doesn't sit right. To ease the discomfort, I holster my terrablade and offer my hand. She ignores it.

'Liv Carson's the name,' she says. She points with her chin towards the dead forest. 'And what we're looking for is in there.'

My hand drops. I look back at the skeletons dangling from the trees. 'The décor certainly gives one pause.'

The woman chuckles and my heart sinks. A sense of humour in a spirit hunter is a telltale sign that they're new to this kind of work, and a clue that they do not yet have a healthy respect for warnings given by the dead.

'Oh, I don't know,' says Liv, smiling. 'It's nice in a dark, stay-the-hell-off-our-planet kind of way.' She lifts her glowing blade and points it towards the trees. 'Shall we go and see if they have the kettle on for us? Upstairs sent me here in a rush this morning and I missed my first coffee.'

I find her levity uncomfortable. It could be the sign of a reckless nature. But I hold my thoughts close.

'Lead the way,' I say.

***

It's cold inside the dead forest. Spectre-plasm leaches from the ground in bright tendrils that spin upward in uncanny spirals. The sand, ribbed and mounded up against the dead trees, is darker here also. Every now and then we pass remains—bones sticking like toothpicks out of the dirt; a dusty Hegemon helmet.

Liv pauses by one of the trees. She uses the tip of her terrablade to dig clear a half-buried body from the foot of it. I frown at her use of the weapon in such a way. The tool of our trade demands respect. Her actions finally reveal the mummified body of a native. Lithe of form, horned, rough skinned and clawed, it looks to be more savage animal than humanoid. But the desiccated gash across its throat shows that it was killed the same as any other living thing can be.

'Look at that,' says Liv. 'Ugly things.'

I shrug. 'Not ugly. Just different. I hear they were a brave race. They fought well. It took twelve Hegemon battalions to see them finished. Not many of our soldiers returned.'

Liv looks impressed. 'I'd never fight for my planet like that. But then again, it's a shithole world on the edge of the Erdani system. All rocks and reptile farms. No-one would be interested in it anyway.'

Not unless they found grey fuel on it, I think as I look at the native and feel a moment's sorrow at the waste of life.

Liv seems to lack any such compassion. Done with the corpse, she glances over her shoulder. 'Anyway, as fun as it is talking about home, I'm more interested in killing something. Let's keep going.'

The trees open out ahead. The piles of dried bodies mound higher. Hegemon and native alike. They carpet the ground, and it takes all my effort to avoid stepping on them. Liv has no such qualms. She takes a direct line to the clearing, crunching her way over the bones. I frown again. Her lack of respect for the dead is disappointing.

The ache in my joints and teeth intensifies as I enter the clearing. Here the sand is no longer orange but dark brown—heavy with old blood. I clench my teeth against the planet's pain. This is where the final stand was made, where the most lives were lost.

From the corner of my eye, I see Liv stumble. She must be feeling the effects of the planet's emotions also.

She sucks in a deep breath. 'By stardust,' she curses. 'Be damned but this planet is angry.'

'Not angry,' I say. 'Anguished.'

Liv looks dubious. 'How can you tell the difference?'

'Think of worlds as mothers,' I say. 'This one has had her children murdered. She is grieving for them.'

Liv scoffs and pushes herself upright. 'It's just a planet.'

I disagree. Perhaps that is the difference between being a priestess and a murderer.

I unsheathe my terrablade and press the activation key on the hilt. My fingers tingle as the metal awakens; light racing down the length of the blade as it blazes to life and phases into the translucent, part gaseous compound that dispels spectre-plasm. The active terralight, coloured red, illuminates the clearing. Liv's blade follows suit. I look into the wall of forest that lines the clearing.

Where are they? Where are the dead?

It doesn't take them long to arrive. The ghosts emerge from the trees like pillars of smoke. Hundreds of them. Their tall, transparent, willow-like forms are clad in bloodstained robes. Their green skin is like roughened bark. Horns, elegantly twisted into crowns, adorn their heads. All are armed with wicked looking spears.

Then I see the elder spirit that leads them. His horns are piled higher and are more elaborately woven than the rest. As he enters the circle of light thrown by the terrablades, I see that his spear is no memory, but made of true steel. I glance back at the others and frown. Every spirit's weapon is the same—very real.

The elder's voice rasps, sounding like sand grating against stone. 'Your step offends. Leave here.'

Liv answers, 'Stay down, shades. This land is no longer yours. Yield.'

I glare at her. Any experienced spirit hunter knows to speak to the dead respectfully.

The elder's teeth grind. 'We will not,' he says, 'without a fight.'

Liv grins. 'More than happy to oblige!'

Before I can defuse the situation, Liv has rammed her blade, tip first, deep into the ground.

'*No!*' I cry. 'Gently! Or the planet will revolt!'

Liv glances at me, her eyes reflecting the red fire of her blade. Her lips peel back. 'Who cares about the damned planet? We're here to kill ghosts—so let's kill them!'

I growl in frustration. It's too late now to try a kinder approach. I whisper an apology to Amarion-5 and press the tip of my own blade into the ground. It slides through like cutting into butter. Then, feeding off the old blood in the earth, the terralight in the blade expands.

A shard of lightning hurtles into the planet's core, seeking to smother its life force. The sudden flux of the world's response hits like a hammer—a wild, desperate wave of ancient emotion that travels through the blade and into my body.

Amarion-5 gathers her deeper resources to attack. I firm my grip on the hilt of the blade. I brace my feet against the desecrated soil.

Bleed-off power from the terrablade coils across the ground. Raw and red, it carves into the ranks of advancing spirits. The ghosts fall to its touch, their screams fading as they crumble to ash.

But it isn't enough. Our work is doomed to failure. The planet fights hard; the phantoms are too numerous.

Not enough time.

I hear a cry. Liv stumbles as the ground at her feet opens. Her offending blade dislodges, leaving broken edges of earth glowing red in triumph.

The planet has given her ghosts the opening they need.

Liv staggers back as the spirits reach her. She cries out, swamped.

I draw my own blade free, releasing the planet's core. I rush to Liv's aid, my boots floundering in the sand as I go.

One metre. Two metres. I'm standing over Liv. I turn the glowing, translucent length of my blade against the horde. Their ghostly flesh presses against the knife's edge and the run of their spectre-plasm slicks my wrists. They are just memories, dying, but the priestess in me screams along with their despair.

This is no way to end the brave dead.

Liv rallies. She rises to fight by my side. Splattered spectre-plasm and the acrid smell of burning terralight surround us. We fight.

We fight.

But still we are failing…

'We need to cage them!' screams Liv as she ducks under the wicked point of a spear. The wielder falls on the edge of her blade. Another spirit takes its place. 'We have no choice!'

I curse, trying to think of an alternative solution. But the ghosts surge forward again, almost overwhelming me. I duck another spear thrust and swallow my reservations. Liv is right. Better to end the already dead than join them.

'I'll go left,' I yell back.

I step to the side and drive the tip of my blade back into the ground. Again I feel the planet's recoil. I ignore the gut-deep feeling that what I am doing is wrong. Then, with the ghosts milling alongside me, I run left, trailing my weapon in the sand.

A slice of light follows the line of the blade. Breathtaking and deadly it rises like a curtain into the desert air. Liv moves in the opposite direction. A fiery terralight glow follows in her footsteps. We will need to meet precisely at the other end to ensure we encircle the shades.

Cage them.

I run. My leg muscles burn but I maintain focus on the end game. The sand drags at the blade and sucks at my feet. I force myself onward. The ghosts realise what is happening. Their strident battle cry raises the hairs on my skin. I take in a deep breath and hope that whatever gods are watching will forgive what we are about to do.

The trees seem to clutch at me as I run. Their spikes bite into my shoulders. Vicious. Blood from a hundred small nicks runs down my arms and legs. I glance over. The glow of Liv's blade keeps pace with me off to the right. The ghosts sprint, trying to overtake us. I speed up and shift direction, circling around to the right.

Moments seem like hours. The ghosts run neck-and-neck with me. I glimpse the elder spirit, his horns glowing red in the light thrown from the blades. His gaze locks onto mine. Condemnation blazes in eyes that glitter like an animal's—green and wicked. *Your choices define you,* his scrutiny seems to say. *Murderer.* Guilt washes through me. Unwilling to hold the weight of his unspoken accusation, I look away.

Liv emerges from the trees to my right. Her face is red, her legs pumping an uneven tattoo across the ground. We are within touching distance as we pass each other, just enough space for the light of our blades to connect.

The elder's unearthly, despairing roar makes me stumble. The wall of his soldiers strikes the terralight barrier. Their screams pierce the air as they are reduced to ash. I turn to look at Liv. Her terrablade lies in the dust as she stands with hands on knees sucking in great breaths of air.

Then I hear another mighty roar. The elder. Over the top of the wall he emerges, the length of his spear used as a vault to clear the barrier. He lands between Liv and me. Before I can help her, the elder raises his spear. Liv only has enough time to stand upright. He plunges his weapon through her chest.

'*No!*' I run, but I'm already too late. The elder roars in victory. A spray of blood coats Liv's lips.

The murderer in me wakes. I shift the grip on my sword, every muscle in my arm tightening. My blade, its length still burning with terralight, drives through the elder's heart.

There is satisfaction in seeing his head fly back in a wordless cry. Satisfaction in watching the terralight eat away at him. In moments his body is a pillar of ash. He crumbles and is gone, motes carried away on the slight breeze.

I kneel by Liv's side. Her eyes are open and her throat works as she struggles to breathe.

'Thrice-damned ghosts,' she whispers. 'I let them get me, didn't I?'

I have nothing useful to say, no words to ease her regret.

'Did we get the rest of them?' she asks.

This I can answer. 'We did. The shades have all been dispersed.'

'The shades have *all* been dispersed?' She laughs. Another bright gush of blood washes across her chin. 'You don't know, do you? I thought maybe you did, that you thought you could trick me. But you really don't...'

I frown. 'What don't I know?'

She laughs again, this time ending on a choking cough. Her eyes squeeze shut and her hands clutch at the haft of the spear protruding from her chest. I place my hand over hers. Her skin is hot against my palm.

She grimaces and pulls away. Her eyes glitter with the light of last life rallied.

'You didn't land on Amarion-5, Cyanna. Your ship crashed.' She bares her bloodied teeth. 'You're dead!'

I leap to my feet. My heart pounds. I look down. My body seems real. Solid. My terrablade is a heavy weight in my grasp.

'I can't be dead...' I stutter. But I don't remember my actual landing. Only the struggle of the descent through Amarion-5's atmosphere, and after that leaving the ship.

And if I still lived, her skin would not have felt so hot to me.

I step away from her, the spectre-plasm leaking rapidly out of her dying body suddenly ominous. Liv turns her head to look at me, her cheek resting against the dark sand. Her gaze, still cold, bores into mine. In her eyes I see she finds my confusion amusing.

Her voice sounds wet, 'You have to admit it was clever of me to use you. A ghost to kill ghosts. Pretty funny, hey?'

But I don't have a sense of humour.

I don't find it funny.

Not funny at all.

My blood rages, boiling through my veins like fire. Darkness creeps in at the edges of my vision. I see, again, the innocent native spirits I just helped to disperse. I step back to Liv's side as life fades from her body. Her shade rises from the ruin of her death. She smiles when she sees me.

'Hey,' she says, flexing her fingers. 'This being dead thing isn't so bad.'

But the murderer in me surfaces again. Hot and searing, my anger burns away the morality of the priestess. I raise my weapon. The red light of its power washes over Liv's face.

'You don't deserve to linger,' I say as I plunge my terrablade through her.

Her eyes widen. Her form fractures and falls to ash.

And, when I lower my blade, it is done.

I am alone—the last left to stand as this planet's protector.

And protect her I will.

Acknowledgments

My thanks to the various editors who have worked with me on the previously published stories in this collection, and also my exceptional beta readers who brave the early drafts and give their welcome feedback. You know who you are.

Thank you also to Lauren and Geneve. Our circle is strength.

And to Aiki Flinthart. How I miss you! I am grateful every day for all you taught me about both writing and life. This collection holds the balance of the stories left that you edited for me, and this project is stronger for the gift of your deft skill.

And most importantly, my heartfelt thanks go to my family. To Darren, Piper and Dakota. You are the source of joy that keeps the stories flowing.

References

'A Pitcher of Water at the End of Days' first appeared in the anthology, *Aquarius (Zodiac Series 2)*, Deadset Press, January 2020

'Rusted Wings' first appeared in the anthology, *Clockwork Dragons: A Fantasypunk Anthology*, Zombie Pirate Publishing, January 2020

'Terralight' first appeared in the anthology, *The Zookeeper's Tales of Interstellar Oddities*, CAT Press, March 2020

'Three Door Saloon' first appeared in the anthology, *Rogues' Gallery: Anthology of Scoundrels*, CAT Press, June 2020

'Mirrorverse' first published on Amazon KDP, Four Ink Press, November 2020

'In Opposition to the Foe' first appeared in the anthology *Relics, Wrecks and Ruins*, CAT Press, January 2021

ABOUT THE AUTHOR

Pamela Jeffs is a speculative fiction author living in Queensland, Australia. Her work has been published in various magazines and anthologies and has been shortlisted for numerous Australian Aurealis Awards and has received both Honorable and Silver Honorable Mentions for the USA Writers of the Future Competition.

The Terralight Collection is her fourth collection.

To discover more books by Pamela Jeffs and be notified of new releases, deals and specials, visit and subscribe at:

www.pamelajeffs.com
Twitter: @Pamela_Jeffs
Facebook: @pamelajeffsauthor

OTHER TITLES

Discover other titles by Pamela Jeffs at:
www.pamelajeffs.com

Including:

Collections

Red Hour and Other Strange Tales
Saloons & Stardust: A Collection
Five Dragons
Turtle Island

Co-Authored Anthologies

The Zookeeper's Tales of Interstellar Oddities

If you enjoyed this book, please go to Goodreads
and/or Amazon and leave a review. It helps
Thank you.

www.ingramcontent.com/pod-product-compliance
Lightning Source LLC
Chambersburg PA
CBHW030432120726
47903CB00003B/924